SUMMER
DANCE

LYNN SWANSON

Go to www.lynnswansonbooks.com to see other books by Lynn Swanson and to arrange for school visits, study guides, readings, and book signings.

To make *Summer Dance* come alive, the author suggests readers listen to the music from the performances in the book, including *Swan Lake, Les Patineurs, Les Sylphides, Nutcracker, Romeo & Juliet,* and the Kronos Quartet's *Pieces of Africa.*

———

———

Acknowledgments

A *grand révérence* and a bouquet of flowers to:

Cameron Basden, Director of Dance, Interlochen Center for the Arts, for her helpful suggestions and joyful response

Sharry Traver Underwood, spirited dancer, dance educator, and writer for her reading, constant friendship, and enthusiastic support

A special bow and a rose from my bouquet to Jess for his support and honor of me and Summer Dance

Dedication

Summer Dance is dedicated to those spirits of dance who inspired me:

My mother, Mary Kay

Joe Kaminsky, Sheila Reilly, Gay Delanghe, and Stephanie Rand

and, of course, to Sara and Eryn

Table of Contents

PART ONE

PART TWO

PART ONE

CHAPTER ONE

"Amazing!"

Sara dropped her dance bag on the nearest bunk. She was finally at Lakewood Dance Camp, and the Pavlova cabin looked pretty cool. I can hardly believe it, she thought— I'll be living in a cabin named after one of the greatest ballerinas who ever lived!

She stood in the center of the room and looked around, glad her mom had left before she ran into her cabin mates. The three double bunks were empty except the bottom one near the bathroom. A yellow flowered bedroll was neatly placed on it, and underneath were a zillion boxes of pointe shoes. Sara had four pairs to last the summer. That's when it hit her—she'd be living in this cabin for the whole summer with strangers. Strangers she'd have to compete against for class placement, dance parts, and for the big prize of being named one of the top three dancers in the Intermediate Division.

She took the wrinkled Lakewood brochure out of her pocket and stared at the picture of last summer's winners in their colorful costumes. *Three dancers in each division win scholarships to return to Lakewood.* She stared, as she had for months, at the dancers' bouquets of flowers and ecstatic faces. Her heart filled with excitement as she folded the brochure and returned it to her pocket.

She eyed the beds near the door. They looked safe, away from the person she didn't know yet. She tossed her purple bedroll onto the top bunk and opened the window next to it, breathing in the northern Michigan pine. Then she sat on the bunk below and rummaged in her dance bag through pointe shoes and ballet slippers, tap and character shoes, leg warmers, and Band-Aids until she touched her lucky locket. She pulled the locket out of its velvet bag and put it on. She just had to win a scholarship.

Next year was her brother's turn to go to soccer camp. There was no way that eleven-year old kicking machine was going to give that up, and there wasn't enough money to send them both someplace in the same summer. Sometimes her dad sent the child support payments and sometimes he didn't, but he did give her the locket. And Miss Abbey, her ballet teacher at home, believed in her talent and wanted her to dance every summer from now on. As Sara unloaded her suitcase of clothes into a drawer, she could hear Miss Abbey telling her how lucky she was that Lakewood—possibly the greatest summer dance program anywhere—was right in her own state. Lakewood could connect Sara to master teachers, excellent training, and the chance to get into a professional ballet company some day. It would be amazing! She closed the drawer, threw the empty suitcase into the closet and wondered how strong the competition would be. Right on cue, the old screened door squeaked open.

CHAPTER TWO

"The Competition and the Friend"

Sara turned to see a strawberry-haired girl in the doorway, long straight legs beneath her shorts. Unless Sara could grow longer legs overnight, this was serious competition by itself.

"I'm Robin Stewart from Chicago," the girl announced as if Sara should already know. She brushed a curl from her face and pitched her expensive dance bag on the bunk under Sara's.

"I'm Sara Sutherland,"—but Robin left, letting the door bang shut. Sara turned her dark eyes into the mirror to check out her light brown hair, then she glanced down at her medium-length legs. Robin quickly reappeared with a bulging suitcase.

"Where are you from?" Robin asked.

"Here," Sara answered. "About five hours south." Robin looked at her like she wanted something more. Sara suddenly wished she were from someplace far away. Connecticut would have been good.

"Oh," Robin said. "I've never seen you at Lakewood before."

"This is my first year," Sara answered.

5

"This is my third," Robin said, sitting on her suitcase. "I'm fourteen. How old are you?"

Sara was starting to feel like a suspect being interrogated. As she said "Thirteen" the door opened again and a tiny girl came in. Her clothes seemed to hang, making her look even smaller. Her hair was so blonde it was white, her eyes light blue. Sara liked her instantly.

"Hi. I'm Erin Christopher." She plopped onto the yellow flowered sleeping bag.

The stranger I was afraid of, Sara thought, wishing she had taken the bunk above her. "I'm Sara and that's Robin," Sara smiled.

Robin nodded as she unzipped her suitcase. Without looking up she asked Erin all her questions starting with, "Where are you from?"

New York City, thirteen, and first time here were the answers. New York! Now there were questions Sara wanted to ask. "Want to go for a walk?" she asked, looking at her watch. "There's a half hour until dinner and the opening session."

"I don't. I want to get organized," Robin said, dumping a pile of leotards onto her bed. Erin shrugged.

"Let's go," Sara said, and soon she and Erin were on a path deep in towering fir trees. "Tell me everything about New York," Sara said excitedly.

"Did you know there's a boys camp across the lake?" Erin asked.

"Yeah," Sara answered. She had seen the sign on the way in—"Camp Will-O-Green." She was sure it would be off-limits. The path narrowed then wound steeply upward, finally spilling them into an opening high over the lake.

"Wow!" was all Sara could say. They were face to face with a breathtaking view of the deep blue lake with its long sandy shore and thick ring of green trees. The clear June sky seemed to have burst above, holding the picture in an azure frame.

"Wow," Erin echoed. They fell onto an old wooden lookout bench and screamed as a little chipmunk scurried out from under it. Then they began to laugh so hard it was as though they had known each other forever.

Sara asked again. "What's it like in New York?"

Erin was busy staring across the lake. "Good. Last year I got to dance *Nutcracker* with the company."

"The company?" Sara said.

"Yeah, the New York City Ballet," Erin said casually as she stood up.

Sara was amazed that it was possible to actually dance with a professional company when you were only thirteen. It was what Miss Abbey wanted for her, why she was at Lakewood. It was why she'd been the babysitter for every kid in town all year to pay for summer dance shoes.

"Look!" Erin pointed into the sunshine, her hand over her eyes.

The boys were on their beach, but Sara couldn't see any faces. She thought of Jason, her boyfriend last year in seventh grade. Her heart fell as she remembered how he had taken someone else to the spring dance because she was busy rehearsing for her dance recital.

"I wonder how you get over there," Erin was saying when the sharp clangs of a dinner bell struck the air.

"Want to run back?" Sara asked, taking off for the path. Erin ran after her, and together they raced down the hill and through the tall trees into the unknown summer.

CHAPTER THREE

"Opening Session"

Chattering girls surrounded Sara and Erin as they stood in the cafeteria line on the dining hall steps. Sara smelled fresh rolls mingled with the scent of warm chocolate. A cool breeze off the lake made her shiver, and she turned to see waves splashing against the dock. But when she stepped inside the door she felt cozy. The dining hall's shiny wood floor, long tables, and high-backed chairs were more beautiful than she expected. It was hard to believe Lakewood was fifty years old. She saw placards in the middle of the tables with the names of each cabin, all famous dancers: Nijinsky, Makarova, Tallchief, Baryshnikov.

"Look!" Erin nodded as they stood with full trays. "There's Pavlova table!"

Sara spotted Robin already at the table, probably asking everyone her questions. Over the din of voices Sara met the rest of her cabin mates. The quiet girl next to her with fluffy brown hair, deep eyes, and dark skin was Danielle Overman from California; the sandy-haired girl with the big smile was Becky Rice from Wisconsin. Robin was engrossed in conversation with a thin, dark-haired girl next to her and Sara could see why. She laughed at everything Robin said, and the two of them had painted on lipstick and mascara.

"This is Hillary Weisman from New Jersey," Robin said. "She's fourteen." "They're all thirteen," she told Hillary. Like fourteen is so much older, Sara thought. Besides, she was thirteen and a half. Erin only shrugged.

As Sara ate her last bite of spaghetti Robin shushed them. "Miss Sutton's going to speak." A roar of shouts and applause rose to the rafters as the camp director stood at the podium, a tall poised woman with shiny black hair. Sara knew from her brochure that Miss Sutton had been a principal dancer in an English ballet company. You couldn't tell how old she was, but Miss Abbey always said dancers were like spirits, so age didn't matter.

"Remember," Miss Sutton said. "There will be competition for class placement, for parts, and for scholarships, but I challenge each of you to strive for growth in character as well as in dance. The qualities we look for in our scholarship winners are leadership, cooperation, enthusiasm, and improvement."

Sara closed her eyes, touched her locket, and repeated the words: *leadership, cooperation, enthusiasm, improvement.*

"He's really cute," Erin said, nudging Sara. Sara looked up to see a handsome young man with curly dark hair. Mr. Moyne would be their tap and folk teacher. Sara wondered if she'd be good in folk class. You'd have to be good in everything to get a scholarship.

Miss Casey stood next, a petite blonde who would be their modern dance instructor. She said she knew some of them had not taken modern yet, and assured them it would be a wonderful new way to move. But Sara didn't think so—she had watched modern dancers throw themselves onto the floor, and she did not have a good feeling about it.

10

Now Miss Sutton introduced her special guest ballet teacher, Madame Landovsky.

Madame stood slowly in a dark dress. She did not smile. Her graying hair was coiled at the back of her head. Sara felt Madame's eyes and had the uneasy feeling that she already knew the level of her dancing, the work that needed to be done.

"Madame danced in Russia," Erin whispered into Sara's ear. "I hear she's tough."

Madame finally spoke. "Thank you. I see you in class" was all she managed to say. And that was in an English Sara could barely understand.

Sara was lost in imagining a young Madame gliding across a vast stage while thousands of hearty Russians applauded wildly and threw flowers at her feet. The next thing she knew, their counselor was at the table introducing herself as Mary Anderson and passing out yellowed song sheets. When she had gone, Sara heard Robin say she was glad that Mary would be three whole cabins away from theirs. Sara wondered what would be going on that Mary shouldn't know about. Miss Sutton motioned for the pianist to begin, and Sara sang with the others:

Lakewood, Lakewood nestled fair
among the leaves and northern air.
We come to you to dance and share,
to grow and learn, to teach and care,
to make new friends and build new paths,
which lead us on to dreams that last.
And when the summer's days are through,
we'll think of our return to you
and never once throughout the year
forget our friends made steadfast here.

Screams and applause shook the room again until Miss Sutton interrupted. "The next time we sing this song will be at the final dance concert in August," she smiled. "In the big outdoor theater on the lake." Her eyes took on a dreamy look. "The three scholarship winners from each division will be announced then." Sara tried to imagine the last day of camp eight weeks away, but could hardly believe it was the first day and that she was really here. Miss Sutton excused them saying, "We'll see you at class placement auditions in the morning."

At the mention of auditions Sara's stomach tightened, but when she went out of the hall and saw fiery orange torches dancing in the wind by the lake and a big yellow moon shining on black water, she melted into the magic.

CHAPTER FOUR

"Audition"

In the morning Sara ran upstairs from the locker room, but stopped short when she saw the dance studio. The huge room overflowed with dancers, their black leotards and pink tights reflected in tall mirrors. "Come on," Erin said, brushing past her. "Let's get a good place at the barre." Sara wanted to move, but felt frozen. Then the accompanist arrived with his sheet music. It was all going to start, ready or not. She ran over to Erin just as Miss Sutton and the teachers came in with their clipboards and pencils. Sara looked at herself in the mirror, straightened her tights, and pushed a piece of loose hair into place.

"Everyone take a deep breath," Miss Sutton smiled, trying to help them relax. Sara obeyed, but her body felt stiff. She shook her hands, trying to loosen her muscles.

"We'll do the barre exercises together then break into small groups for center-floor and pointe work," Miss Sutton said. "You will know before you leave whether you're in Class A or B."

Sara knew from the brochure that Class A was the advanced group. She just had to make it. When the audition numbers were given out in alphabetical order, Sara pinned number 48 to the front of her leotard and took her place at the barre between Robin and Hillary who seemed to tower over her. She was wondering how they'd all have enough room to move when Miss Sutton began pliés. On the tendu exercise Sara made a mistake, and her foot nearly crashed into Robin's. She looked at the judges whose faces revealed nothing. But Robin shot her a look as they turned to repeat the exercise on the other side. It could have been disaster. She reached to touch her locket, but remembered it wasn't there, that they weren't allowed to wear any jewelry with their dance clothes.

Sara was best at the slow adage work, so when her group was called to do it, she ran center-floor to take a place in the front line. But Robin went for the same spot, and there were too many dancers in front when the music began. No one budged, so Sara quickly moved to the back.

The allégro, or quick chain of steps, was always the hardest part of class for Sara, and today's combination looked impossible. Though she watched carefully as the first groups performed the tricky steps and crossing of ankles in air, she knew she should stay in the back line. But Robin kept behind her this time. The lines were lopsided with three dancers in front and five in back. "Come on," Miss Sutton said. "Move up. Come to the front." Sara thought Miss Sutton was looking at her. Robin stayed glued to the floor behind Sara and whispered for her to move up. Miss Sutton was still staring, so Sara ran to the front line.

The music pushed Sara faster and faster, and when the girl next to her fell apart in the middle of the exercise, Sara nearly did too. She forced herself to look into the mirror to keep up with the dancers who were doing it well, including Robin.

They had already been dancing an hour and a half—the length of an entire class at Sara's home studio, and Miss Sutton had no intention of stopping.

"Both hands on the barre, rises onto pointe," Miss Sutton said when the class had put on pointe shoes. Sara turned square to the barre. She knew the pointe work by itself could separate the dancers. She worked hard to keep up with the fast pace of rises, quick leg changes, and shifts in direction.

Then it was quiet except for the teachers' murmurs as they compared notes. Finally Miss Sutton said, "Will the following dancers please sit at the side of the room..." Sara shuttered as twelve numbers were called, but she and Erin were safe.

Miss Sutton instructed them to organize by pairs, take four steps across the floor, rise on pointe into arabesque and hold the back leg up as long as the music demanded. Sara and Erin lined up to dance across the big room together. "Ready?" Erin whispered. Sara pressed each of her pointes into the rosin box to keep from slipping. She took a deep breath and stepped out from the corner with Erin. "Step onto a straight leg," she remembered Miss Abbey saying. "Shoulders square." But on the last arabesque she felt her arm pull her off balance and was too tired to correct it. She slid off her pointe shoe and recovered by striking a pose. At first she thought no one noticed, but then saw Madame glancing her way and making a note.

After the last pair danced, the audition seemed to end. The instructors gathered in a group while the dancers stood wearily at the barres. Miss Casey whispered and pointed to the dancers while Mr. Moyne nodded his head and Madame frowned. Then Miss Sutton asked six more dancers to sit out. Becky was out, but the rest of her cabin was still in the running for Class A. Sara sighed and waited for the next instruction.

"From the corner, please," Miss Sutton said. "Turns across the floor. Three singles and a double. One dancer at a time."

Sara couldn't believe it. She wasn't even sure she could do a double traveling turn on pointe. She watched Erin leave the corner and reach the end of the room, then felt all eyes turn to her. Her legs felt weak, like they belonged to someone else. She was sure they would not hold her up or help her turn. But this could be her last chance to make Class A. She breathed deeply, felt a spark of energy, and took off.

She reached the end of the room leaving a trail of mostly solid turns behind her, and looked back at the long path she had completed over the blond wood floor. It was unbelievable. She saw Erin's smile across the room and ran over to her, inspired by her own performance.

"Thank you, girls. Please sit quietly." Miss Sutton led the instructors out of the studio into her office.

It's all over, Sara thought, feeling both safe and scared. Her toes were throbbing and she wanted a drink from the shiny silver fountain in the hall. But she took her cue from Erin and sat on the floor with the others, too tired to whisper. Just when Sara began to relax, the teachers returned. It's final now, she thought.

"If you hear your number, come center-floor," Miss Sutton said. She began calling out numbers in no particular order, and Hillary was called with some others. When Sara heard her number and left Erin to join the group, her heart sank at the possibility that they would be in different classes, with Sara in Class B. But when Robin was called to join her group, Sara knew it had to be Class A. And when the last number was called and Erin joined them, Sara nearly burst in excitement.

16

"Class A," Miss Sutton announced, looking at Sara's group. "And Class B," she finished, turning to the others. Sara felt her heart soar as high in the air as any ballerina had ever leaped.

CAMP LAKEWOOD

INTERMEDIATE DIVISION

CLASS A

JUNE 26 - AUGUST 27

MONDAY	9:00-10:30 Ballet Studio B Madame Landovsky	10:45-12:00 Tap Studio C Mr. Moyne	12:00-1:00 -LUNCH-	2:30-3:40 Modern Dance Studio A Miss Casey	3:45-5:00 Folk Dance Studio C Mr. Moyne		5:30-6:30 -DINNER-	Rehearsal May Be Called
TUESDAY	8:30-10:00 Pointe Studio B Madame Landovsky	10:45-12:00 Folk Dance Studio C Mr. Moyne	12:00-1:00 -LUNCH-	2:00-3:30 Ballet Studio B Madame Landovsky	3:50-5:15 Modern Dance Studio A Miss Casey		5:30-6:30 -DINNER-	Rehearsal May Be Called
WEDNESDAY	9:00-10:30 Ballet Studio B Madame Landovsky	10:45-12:00 Tap Studio C Mr. Moyne	12:00-1:00 -LUNCH-	2:30-3:40 Modern Dance Studio A Miss Casey	3:45-5:00 Folk Dance Studio C Mr. Moyne		5:30-6:30 -DINNER-	Rehearsal May Be Called
THURSDAY	8:30-10:00 Pointe Studio B Madame Landovsky	10:45-12:00 Folk Dance Studio C Mr. Moyne	12:00-1:00 -LUNCH-	2:30-3:40 Ballet Studio B Madame Landovsky	3:45-5:00 Modern Dance Studio A Miss Casey		5:30-6:30 -DINNER-	Rehearsal May Be Called
FRIDAY	9:00-10:30 Ballet Studio B Madame Landovsky	10:45-12:00 Tap Studio C Mr. Moyne	12:00-12:45 -LUNCH-	1:00-2:30 Pointe Studio B Madame Landovsky	2:40-3:40 Modern Dance Studio A Miss Casey	3:50-5:00 Folk Dance Studio C Mr. Moyne	5:30-6:30 -DINNER-	
SATURDAY				NO CLASSES. REHEARSAL MAY BE CALLED.				
SUNDAY				NO CLASSES. REHEARSAL MAY BE CALLED.				

- BREAKFAST IS SERVED BETWEEN 6 A.M. AND 8 A.M. -

CHAPTER FIVE

"The Lifeguard"

A fter lunch, Sara and Erin went back to the empty cabin. They sat on Erin's bunk examining the schedule: *Camp Lakewood Intermediate Division - Class A: June 26-August 27.*

"Look at this," Erin said. "We're going to be in class all day nearly every day."

Sara looked over the schedule. "Yeah. I've never taken more than three classes a week," she said, excited at the prospects of dancing so much all summer.

"Me neither," Erin said. "And I've never taken a tap lesson in my life."

Sara suddenly felt how sore her muscles were. "Uhhhg," she groaned, falling backward on Erin's bed. "I'll never dance again." They were laughing when Danielle and Becky came in.

"Hey you guys," Becky said. "Congrats on making Class A."

"Yeah," Danielle echoed. "Congrats." The door swung open and Robin and Hillary came in dripping in wet bathing suits.

"Come on!" Hillary said.

19

"What's going on?" Danielle asked.

"Water test!" Hillary said. "If you can tread water for twenty minutes, you pass, and you can go out to the raft and take a boat out. We already passed."

"Cool," Danielle said. She and Becky got their suits.

"I think I'll take it tomorrow," Sara said. The truth was, she wasn't that great a swimmer. Since she was five, all her spare time had been spent in the dance studio. She wasn't sure she could even stay afloat twenty minutes.

"OK, then you'll have to wade at the beach like a baby," Robin said. "Come on," she said to Hillary, opening the door. Becky and Danielle quickly followed.

Mary opened the cabin door. "Let's go!" she called. "Water test!"

"OK," Erin answered. "We're coming." There was no choice. Before she knew it, Sara was in water over her head while a cute lifeguard from Camp Will-O-Green counted down the time. The first ten minutes seemed to go quickly but then she got tired.

"Just let yourself float," the lifeguard shouted, his light hair glistening in the sun.

Sara let her arms go out from her and dropped her head back, but the water was icy on her scalp. She decided to make her way over to Erin at the far edge of the ropes. Erin was splayed on top of the lake like a spider, her white hair floating around her. "How much time do you think is left?" Sara asked.

"Not too much," Erin answered calmly. "How old do you think the lifeguard is?" Sara managed to turn so she could see him. Robin was busy chatting with him.

"Four more minutes!" he yelled, pointing to his watch. He might as well have said four more hours. Sara turned onto her back and pretended to be in a water ballet, but it didn't help. "I'm going back," she told Erin.

"Don't give up, Sara," Erin said. "We're almost done."

"I won't," Sara promised.

"Two more minutes," the lifeguard hollered out to her holding up two fingers.

Sara felt weary, and the water began to get choppy. It hit the back of her head and waved into her face. Come on, she thought, shivering, time must be up. But the lifeguard was still talking with Robin.

Another wave smacked her in the face and as she tried to spit water out, she swallowed more. She realized too late that her whole head had gone under. She managed to kick her legs, then felt her head break the surface. At the same time, she felt the lifeguard's strong arms around her, pulling her back to the dock. She felt him lay her on the sandy wood, and the next thing she knew she was coughing and spitting up water. Her body felt limp.

"I'm OK," she told the faces staring above her, but her throat and nose felt sore.

"Come on," Mary said, getting her to her feet. "Let's get you dressed."

Sara felt stupid. Everyone was looking at her like she had nearly drowned. She would have made it, she knew, if the lifeguard hadn't pulled her out. Knees shaking, she let Mary take her back to the cabin.

Erin came in as Mary left. "Look!" Erin said, opening her hand to show Sara a swim card with a shiny star on it.

"Good for you," Sara told Erin.

"It's yours!" Erin smiled.

Sara looked at the card again. She saw her name on it. "I passed?"

"Yep! Time was just up when you went under."

"I knew it!" Sara took the card.

At dinner that night Robin came up to Sara next to the iced tea machine. "It's too bad you didn't pass the swim test," she said. "It's going to be fun out on the raft."

"Oh, I passed," Sara told her.

"You did?" Robin looked surprised. "Oh," she said, letting ice clink into her glass. "You must have impressed David."

"David?"

"The lifeguard," Robin said.

"I didn't do it on purpose," Sara said, but Robin had already walked away.

CHAPTER SIX

"Madame's First Class & Spooky Slaps"

In the morning Sara curtsied to Madame and walked through the studio door to her first Lakewood lesson. Sunshine flooded the room and painted the wood floor in a crystal-morning clarity that made her ready to begin. She took a place at the barre behind Erin and put her left hand on the rounded wood. She put her heels together and spread her feet into first position. Just as Madame shut the door and announced pliés, the door opened again and someone darted across the room and squeezed into a place at the barre.

"In my class," Madame glared, "door close exactly at nine o'clock. No one to enter after door close." She stared at the late-comer. The dancers stood very still. Sara could feel Erin breathing. She shuttered at the thought of the door slamming in her own face.

"We begin," Madame said. During pliés, Madame visited Sara with a cane. She gently touched the front of Sara's knees, urging them wider over her toes as she rose from the bottom of a plié in second position. "Coming up hardest part," she said to the whole class. "Press knees back. Don't lose turnout." Sara

23

felt herself stiffen from the unexpected attention. Although she knew that corrections to one dancer were meant for every dancer, she hoped Madame had noticed someone else not doing it perfectly.

In each barre exercise that began in fifth position, Madame nudged their heels with her cane if she thought anyone could get a tighter fit from hips to knees to toes. This was new for Sara, as were many of the movements they did away from the barre. At the end of the hour and a half, Sara was relieved when they took their bows—grand révérence—applauded the accompanist, and escaped Madame's watchful stare and many corrections.

In the locker room they had only five minutes to change into their tap shoes and get down the hall to Mr. Moyne. "How did you like class?" Erin asked as Sara threw her ballet slippers into her locker.

"I don't know. Those body positions were strange, and she makes you turn out so much." Sara pulled her tap shoes out of her dance bag. One of the other girls laughed and said, "I didn't know *what* was going on in that class!"

"It's not funny," Robin announced. "You can get demoted to Class B."

"Oh, it couldn't be that bad," Erin said.

"That's what you think," Robin warned.

Tap was OK, but modern dance was another story. A miracle was going to have to happen for Sara to look good in there. It wasn't that she didn't like it, just that it was so different from ballet: bare feet, falling off center posture, recovering, rolling on the floor.

Cozy in her bedroll that night, Sara thought about how strange Madame's class had seemed that day. She worried about her turnout and the Russian body positions. She felt frustrated about modern class, and wondered what her first pointe class with Madame would be like in the morning. She finally turned over and closed her eyes, feeling the locket around her neck. At the same time something crashed against the window next to her head. She held her breath, afraid to move, and realized everyone else in the cabin was asleep.

BANG! Another smack on the glass. She froze. Then a tremendous clap of thunder broke overhead and wind roared through the trees. Terrified, she opened the curtain just a slit. A huge pine tree branch smacked against the window in her face. She swallowed a scream and let the curtain go. She felt under her pillow for her flashlight. When she found it she held it tightly, and when her heart finally beat normally, she fell asleep.

CHAPTER SEVEN

"Madame's Challenge"

Sara woke to Erin's voice and the sound of rain hitting the roof. She was still holding her flashlight. "Sara, it's almost eight o'clock!" Erin was holding her wristwatch. "The alarm didn't go off. Hurry!"

She glanced at the clock, but it was blank. The storm had knocked out the electricity during the night. She pictured Madame's door slamming shut in her face. Drawers were banging closed and pajamas flying through the air as everyone rushed to get ready. Sara jumped down from her bunk, opened her drawer, and grabbed the first leotard she felt.

"I can't find my tights!" Hillary screamed.

Danielle threw herself up onto Hillary's bunk and yanked open the curtains next to her bed letting in what little light there was. Then the light bulb hanging from the ceiling came on, and the clock began to flash "12:00" over and over. It was as though they were in stage lights dancing some weird choreography. Sara ran for the bathroom and had barely finished splashing water on her face when Becky and Robin squeezed in. She hurried out, pulled her jeans over her dance clothes,

27

threw her shoes on, and grabbed her dance bag. Erin took their raincoats off the hooks as Sara reached for her elastic band and bobby pins.

They raced to the dining hall. A dancer had to have food for fuel, no matter what. Sara downed some juice and toast, eyeing the clock. She kept sticking bobby pins into the bun she had made in her hair. They dodged the puddles on the path to the dance building, threw their raincoats into their lockers, got their pointe shoes, and ran down the hall to the studio. Sara didn't breathe again until she took her place at the barre. Robin and Hillary ran in at the last possible moment, and the studio door clicked shut. Madame looked them over like they were her troops. Sara stood stiffly at attention in first position.

"You are..." Madame's voice was next to Sara's ear.

"Sara," she answered with a weak smile.

"No jewels in class," Madame said. "Like rule says."

Oh, my gosh! Sara thought. She had forgotten in the rush to take off her locket! Feeling even stiffer, she quickly took it off and placed it in Madame's open hand. Madame said nothing more, just walked back to the piano, dropped the locket on it and began class. Sara feared she would never be forgiven.

But as the music surrounded her, Sara relaxed into the barre exercises. She soon felt Madame's cane pressing the back of her thigh. "Pull up," Madame said. Sara tried to pull her leg muscles harder, only to feel Madame's hand on her stomach. "Here," Madame told her. "Tight here." Sara quickly tightened the muscles beneath Madame's hand and surprised herself by balancing on her pointe shoes without even touching the barre. Wow! She could have balanced forever. Madame only nodded and moved down the barre.

Center-floor, Madame worked them hard on bourrées, the little running steps on the tips of the pointe shoes. "Bourrée steps to be so tiny is like floating, and so soft is like tip-toe barefoot," Madame instructed. "Quiet, quiet, small whisper of feet."

Sara and Erin waited in line as the dancers began across the floor one at a time. The ceiling creaked with the weight of the Senior Division girls dancing above them, and rain pounded against the big windows.

When Sara was halfway across the floor, Madame clapped her hands for the music to stop. She placed her cane a little ahead of Sara's front foot. "Now you make feet go twice as fast, but not go in front of cane." Sara felt self-conscious. She didn't know if she could do it. Her toes felt pinched and her blister hurt in spite of the Band-Aid covering it. But Madame signaled for the music to begin, and Sara did the steps as quickly as she could against the cane pressing her front foot.

"This better," Madame said without smiling. But before Sara could make it to the end, Madame clapped her hands and the music stopped again. "You pull up," Madame directed. Sara remembered the spot Madame had touched with her hand, and tightened her stomach muscles. But it wasn't enough.

"You *up* on your shoes, but not *out* of your shoes. Please to pull up *out* of your shoes, out of your hips." Madame acted as though she knew Sara could do it. But Sara felt flustered. It was hard to remember everything at once. Robin stared at her. Hillary looked at the floor. The piano started again. Sara got back up on her pointes, positioned her arms, and tried to look pleasant. She pulled up every muscle in her body as tightly as she could, took the tiniest, softest steps she could muster, and ignored the painful blister.

When she made it to Erin's friendly face at the other end of the room, she waited for Madame's comment but Madame was already watching the next girl.

At the end of class Madame spoke to them as they stood perspiring in the center of the room. Sara could feel her hair frizzing from the humidity as the rain continued to hit the windows in a steady sheet. "Senior Division to perform ballet called *Les Sylphides* in four weeks for whole camp and for visiting members of San Francisco Ballet. They perform in Balanchine Theater with orchestra from Lakewood Music School. There is chance for some of you to be in." Sara heard the girls behind her gasp in delight. "All white costumes. Is about light, airy fairies dancing in moonlight for handsome man. Very beautiful and poetic. To Chopin music. And San Francisco Ballet dance something for you."

The San Francisco Ballet! San Francisco was so far away from home Sara didn't think she'd ever get to see anything of them but pictures in dance magazines. Now they'd be dancing right in front of her in the theater named for the dance legend, George Balanchine. And she had a chance to dance for them. Her stomach jumped. First from the possibility that she might be chosen, and then from the heavy weight of how terrible she had just been in class.

"I teach you more bourrée and other parts of ballet," Madame told them. "A few only. Must be strong and soft. Grand révérence now."

As they took their bows, Sara looked into the mirror. But instead of seeing the class, she saw beautiful ballerinas in white costumes under magical lights swirling in the poetic softness of *Les Sylphides*. She could hear the music and see herself dancing in the middle of it. Then the mirror reflected reality again and she saw only her own image: a tired girl with frizzy hair in a blue leotard without a locket. She felt her classmates all around her, and she wondered which of them would be on stage dancing in front of the San Francisco Ballet.

CHAPTER EIGHT

"The Secret Path"

Sara turned a page in her dance magazine while another burst of rain showered the trees outside Pavlova cabin. Three days of rain is long enough, she complained to herself. She was tired of spending her breaks in the cabin and avoiding puddles on the paths. She turned another page and came to an impressive photo of a handsome male dancer leaping in the air. The caption identified him as San Francisco Ballet principal dancer Yuri Pashchenko. "Wow! Erin, look at this," she said, but Erin was writing a letter with a pillow over her head. She looked at Danielle on the bunk under Becky, but Danielle was engrossed in a book. She stared at the inspiring photo, hoping Yuri would be part of the group of San Francisco Ballet dancers coming to Lakewood. Then the door swung open and Robin and Hillary came in.

"Where were you guys?" Danielle asked.

"Nowhere," Robin answered, throwing back the hood of her wet slicker.

"Come on," Danielle said. "You two are always gone during breaks. You go *somewhere.*" Erin took the pillow off her head and looked at Robin and Hillary.

"Yeah," Sara said. "Where do you go?" She watched their faces for a clue. Hillary looked ready to pop with news. Robin shot her a "don't tell" look, but it was too late.

"We took a secret path to the boys camp," she blurted.

"Hillary!" Robin said.

"Well, it's not a big deal or anything—just a little path," Hillary said, taking off her wet shoes. "But we're not telling anybody where it is."

"Come on," Becky urged. "Tell us. We'll decide if it's a big deal or not."

"If you don't tell, I don't believe," Danielle said, going back to her book.

"Yeah," Sara agreed. "It's easy just to say something." She was good at using her own imagination and knew its power. Erin put the pillow back over her head. Sara turned over onto her stomach and leafed through her magazine. Before Becky could look the other way, Robin spoke.

"OK. But everybody has to promise not to tell," Robin said. Becky paid attention, Danielle closed her book, and Erin put down her pillow. Sara sat up and listened. They all stared at Robin. But all they got was a description of a place with horses, a bonfire pit, and little sailboats at the beach.

"So, that's *it*?" Danielle asked.

"Where is this secret path?" Sara asked.

Hillary started to speak, but Robin's look stopped her this time. "It's over by the lake," Robin said casually. "By the tall pine trees."

"Right," Becky laughed. "Like there aren't big pine trees everywhere."

Danielle sighed, tired of the game. She glanced at the clock before opening her book again. "Hey! Break's over!"

Sara looked at the clock. "Uh-oh! Modern class in ten minutes." She joined the scramble to gather her things and get out of the cabin. As she ran down the path to the dance studio, she imagined she was stealing quickly down the secret path to the boys camp cloaked in the thick covering of the trees.

CHAPTER NINE

"The Choice"

"Miss Sutton to watch today," Madame said as Sara stood in her pink satin shoes and gauzy skirt, ready for her fifth pointe class to begin. Madame had not returned the locket and Sara could not get up the courage to ask for it. Miss Sutton sat on a folding chair in front of the mirrors holding a clipboard and pen. It reminded Sara of auditions on the first day. Then she understood—this was the day some of them would be chosen for *Les Sylphides*! She pulled herself up tall.

Madame stopped next to Sara during the adage work at the barre. The slow exercise with the leg moving in the air from front to side and back left plenty of time for a teacher to notice everything. Sara felt Miss Sutton stare at her as she stepped forward onto her pointe shoe and raised her back leg in arabesque. She felt Madame touch her back heel gently and raise it slightly higher. Then she felt the cane running along the underside of her raised leg, checking it for straightness. Sara held the air in her lungs and pulled up all her muscles trying to sustain the pose without leaning against the barre.

Center-floor, Sara was placed in the front line for pirouettes. "Just three slow singles each side," Madame instructed. "Just," Sara thought. It was not easy to do three perfect single turns in a row. As usual, Sara's turns were better to the right than to the left, and though none was perfect, she got through them all without falling off pointe. Madame offered no comments, but clapped her hands announcing, "Bourrées from the corner!"

Sara was afraid as she remembered the first pointe class when her bourrées were a disaster. But today they were to do the step in pairs, and Madame paired Sara and Erin. To Sara's delight, they danced like identical twins—they easily kept their footwork and arms together and even held their end poses for the same length of time.

Finally, Madame gave them a waltz step that ended in a grand jeté, or leap, to the front with arms outstretched, a step from *Les Sylphides*. Sara smiled as the music filled the room, stretched her legs as far and as straight as she could in the leaps, and breathed in at the top of the movement as Miss Abbey had taught her.

Then it was over. "Thank you very much," was all Madame said. Miss Sutton smiled at the class as they filed past her on the way out of the studio.

"I feel like I just danced a whole performance," Erin said wearily on the way to the locker room. It was exceptionally quiet as they changed for folk class.

"Have you noticed how good she is?" Sara whispered to Erin, nodding toward Robin. Though Sara had tried to focus entirely on her own dancing, she couldn't help noticing Robin's strong technique and grace.

"You're good too, Sara," Erin said. "You just have to know it."

"But Madame corrects me all the time!" Sara whispered. She felt she might cry.

Erin looked her straight in the eye. "That is because she sees potential." She pronounced each word distinctly as if to say Sara must be stupid for not understanding that.

"Really?" Sara asked.

"Really," Erin said confidently. Sara let Erin's hopeful words carry her off to folk class, though she felt there might be a price to pay for having potential. Throughout the class, she could not stop thinking about whether she had made it into *Les Sylphides*. She was so full of its possibility, she was afraid she might collapse into a heap like an airless balloon if she didn't make it. But how could she make it without her locket?

As she left the dance building with Erin and headed for lunch, Hillary caught up to them. "Have you checked the bulletin board?" she asked. "The names for *Sylphides* are posted!" She darted past them toward the dining hall.

Sara's feelings were a swirl. She wanted to see and she didn't want to see. She knew she had made it and she knew she hadn't made it. There was no way to prepare for the outcome. Erin grabbed her arm and they started back for the dance building.

Sara bobbed her head around behind the crowd of dancers trying to read the list. She saw it was short—only five names from the Intermediate Division. She saw "Christopher, Erin" at the top and squeezed Erin's arm. "You made it!" She saw "Jacobs, Kathy," in the middle. Then, realizing the list was alphabetical, she held her breath and let her eyes fall to the bottom. But Erin had already done that.

"You made it too!" Erin exclaimed.

"I can't believe it," was all Sara could say as she stared at "Sutherland, Sara" in black ink just above "Tan, Lin," and just below "Stewart, Robin." A note announced that rehearsals would begin the next evening. She would be dancing in front of members of the San Francisco Ballet in just three weeks!

CHAPTER TEN

"Discovering the Boys"

Sara was on the raft after lunch when Erin popped up from the water. "Hey!" Sara said. "I thought you were going to stay in the cabin and read until class."

"I was," Erin said, climbing on the raft. "But it must be a hundred degrees in there."

"What are you reading, anyway?" Sara asked.

"It's a romance about this girl who's a senior in high school. She has a boyfriend who is really cool and everything, but he wants more than kisses, if you know what I mean."

Sara knew what she meant, but didn't want to imagine it. She hadn't even made it to the spring dance. "Do you have a boyfriend?" she asked Erin.

"Yeah, sort of. Justin and I—" But Robin and Hillary climbed onto the raft laughing.

Sara wondered how much they'd heard. "Come on," she said to Erin, getting up. "Let's go." The lookout bench was the only place for a private conversation. They dove off the raft toward the dock and resurfaced next to David.

"Hey, how are you?" David smiled at Sara, putting his sun goggles on top of his head.

Sara felt uneasy, remembering the rescue. She smiled back, looking into his blue eyes. He was definitely sixteen. "Fine," she said. "I never got to thank you."

"That's OK," David said. "All in a day's work." He turned around to stop some horseplay, then turned back to Sara and smiled.

"Well, thanks again," Sara said, walking away with Erin.

They sat on the hilltop bench in the warm summer air. A breeze rustled the fern around them as they gazed down at the beach and the splashing swimmers. Sailboats from Lakewood and Will-O-Green dotted the blue water. Something caught Sara's eye a few yards down the slope to her right. The tangle of underbrush and fern was moving.

"Look!" she whispered. Erin stood up. The brush moved again. Sara saw something brown among the green, and moved quietly toward it. The minute she spread the tangled underbrush and stepped inside the green cover, a little deer darted away, its white tail bobbing downhill into the thicket. Sara wanted to run after it, to discover its adventures.

"Wow!" Erin said behind her. "It's neat in here."

Sara looked around and felt wrapped in green silence. She looked up and saw an umbrella of giant pine trees. She looked down and saw the beginnings of a barely visible path. "This is the secret path to the other side!" she exclaimed. If they went quickly, they might have enough time to take it to the boys camp and get back in time for class.

They took off through the trees on a path so narrow they could hardly keep their bare feet on it. "Ouch!" Erin gasped. Sara turned back to see Erin trying to pull a picker out of her foot. Trouble was, she was balancing in a patch of poison ivy. Great, she thought, realizing that Erin wouldn't recognize the plant. Well, it wouldn't do any good to tell her now; maybe she'd be lucky enough not to break out in the horrible itchy blisters. Erin gave her the "all clear" and they continued on the trail. They were getting into the middle of nowhere, winding downhill around the end of the lake.

As they continued downward, the dry path turned into damp black earth, cool under their feet. Sara smelled the strong fragrance of wild mint and saw the deer drinking from a stream. She felt muck ooze between her toes as the deer took off and Erin started to wade in. But a garter snake slithered along the dark bank.

"Yuk," Erin winced, jumping out of the water. They spotted an old plank thrown across the water downstream and scrambled onto it. As they made their way across, Sara could feel Erin's weight ahead of her making the board sink in the middle. It was definitely a one-person plank. She jumped onto land as soon as she could.

As the path angled upward it became dry again and they followed it to a place where the sun finally broke through the trees. Straight ahead they could see the back of the boys' cabins. They crept quietly forward among thick brush. "It must be getting late," Sara whispered, but Erin pointed ahead. Sara looked and saw boys everywhere swimming, clinking horseshoes, and tossing firewood into the pit. Her eyes were drawn to a dark-haired boy cleaning a little sailboat, his back muscles rippling as he pushed a cloth back and forth. He looked as committed to the boat as Sara was to dancing. Sara watched as he stood and gave the boat a long stare.

"Sara!" Erin whispered. "We gotta go. Everyone's left our beach!"

Sara looked past the boy and across the lake to see the raft still and empty. Everyone had left for class. "Let's go," she said. They ran as fast as they could, sure no one had seen them. It was three days before the ugly poison ivy blisters appeared on Erin's legs.

CHAPTER ELEVEN

"First Rehearsal"

Sara was so excited, she arrived early for the first evening rehearsal of *Les Sylphides*, but she found the room already filled with long-legged Senior Division dancers quietly stretching. Posters of the ballet were mounted on the studio walls, and Sara stared at the dancers in long white costumes posing, leaping, and twirling on the shiny paper. Robin came in, glanced Sara's way, and stood across the room near three seniors. Sara recognized them as the ecstatic faces from the Lakewood brochure—last year's intermediate scholarship winners! Sara was eager to see them dance, but was worried that she wouldn't be able to keep up.

"Had to go to the nurse for the poison ivy," Erin explained as she rushed to take a place next to Sara at the barre. Sara saw a bandage under Erin's tights.

Mr. Moyne came in, Madame arrived, Miss Sutton nodded to the accompanist, and the warm-up began. As she moved them center-floor to set the opening pose, Miss Sutton pointed to the poster near the piano. "This will be our opening and closing pose," she said. Sara looked at the graceful young women in various positions surrounding the single male dancer. It was like a dream, like a suspension of time in a different world. She wondered which dancer she was to be. Mr. Moyne would obviously be the single male dancer. Miss Sutton reminded them of the history of the ballet, telling them that they would dance *Les Sylphides* from start to finish exactly as the famous Russians, Pavlova and Nijinsky, had danced it with their company in the early 1900s.

Madame and Miss Sutton worked quickly to place everyone in the classic pose. From her position across the group from Erin, Sara looked into the mirror. Even with the dancers in rag-tag leotards, sweaters, and warm-up tights, the setting looked beautiful and exactly like the poster. Mr. Moyne was in the center with one dancer lying in front of him on her side in a pretty arch, her head nearly touching her toe. Other girls stood around him at different heights, their heads slightly tilted toward each other. It felt old-fashioned to Sara, but in a good way, like having tea with her grandmother.

"The style of this ballet, the way you feel it and express it, is almost more important than the steps," Miss Sutton said, changing the places of two girls. "It must be danced with an elegance representing the time in which it was choreographed. You are upholding tradition."

Sara stiffened a bit as Madame walked around adjusting heads and arms. "Is good, yes. Now must soften. Must suspend. Is like dream of fairies." Sara stood taller and tried to soften her arms. But Madame didn't like it. "No, not stand too tall. In this ballet, posture lower." She gently pushed Sara into a deeper plié and moved her shoulders forward a bit. As Madame looked her over, Sara tried to feel the exact position so she could do it on her own next time.

She soon understood why they had practiced the little bourrée steps so much in class. The steps had to carry them all the way to the sides of the stage as the group split in half from the opening pose. Sara tried to do the bourrées as quickly and softly as the seniors, but after they had repeated the movement three times, her toes were getting sore, and she wondered how she'd manage to dance on pointe for the entire ballet with such demanding choreography. Luckily, for the next section of the ballet they stood flat in an arabesque pose facing off stage.

"From hip!" Madame's voice demanded in Sara's ear, her hand on Sara's leg. "Turn out from hip, down to foot." Sara quickly obeyed, feeling the movement in her joint.

"Now," Miss Sutton said, "let's take it from the beginning with the music." Madame watched carefully as the dancers took the opening pose. "We'll do it full out," Miss Sutton said, "so we can see what we've got." Sara felt like she had been doing it full out, but when the romantic waltz music began she realized she had more to give. She turned out carefully from the hip during the arabesque pose. But Madame took Sara's arms this time and slowed her movement, changing the energy and shape. "Like this," Madame told her. "Must be so soft." Sara tried to understand. "Don't think no one see you because you not soloist. *Everyone* see you," Madame warned.

Sara felt tired and like she'd never be the dancer she wanted to be. She'd already danced the entire day, she reminded herself, though she knew that was what real dancers did. Then she remembered Erin saying that the better dancers get the corrections. And just the fact that I'm in this at all is a point toward winning a scholarship, she reminded herself. But she worried that if she didn't perform well, it might be a point against her.

"Okay," Miss Sutton finally said, asking them to clear the floor. But instead of excusing them, Miss Sutton began auditioning some of the seniors for solo parts. Sara watched carefully as the older dancers were called to try the grand leaps, the beautiful adage, and the romantic dance for a man and woman, the pas de deux, shown in the posters. Her spirit soared—this was going to be the best performance she had ever been in.

After the large solo auditions, there was a chance for a few other dancers to try for small parts. The ballet would be made up of mostly individual solo dancers with the group ensemble making a backdrop of wonderful, shifting poses. Some seniors got to try for a small part with Mr. Moyne. He ran out to meet the dancer center-stage, waltzed forward with her, then swept her high in the air to each side before carrying her off stage in an overhead lift. Sara's heart danced with the seniors. How wonderful it would feel to be suspended in the air that way!

Then Robin was called to try the part. She wasn't a senior— could she really be chosen? Sara looked at Erin who shrugged, then turned to watch Robin. There was magic from the beginning. Robin seemed to flow into Mr. Moyne's arms. She breathed at the right moments, timing her pliés so Mr. Moyne lifted her effortlessly. She stretched her long legs so far apart in the air over Mr. Moyne's head as he carried her off stage that everyone applauded.

As she watched Robin walk back into the group, Sara heard her own name called! Miss Sutton's hand was ready to start the music. Mr. Moyne stood ready for her. She quickly ran out to the floor, put her right toe back, rounded her arms at her sides, and waited for the music to begin. Be calm, she told herself. Think. When the music began, she waltzed forward. But when Mr. Moyne picked her up for the first lift, it felt awkward. When he bent to lift her the second time, he whispered for her to take a deeper plié. Sara felt confused and realized in that second how much more difficult dancing actually was than it looked. She tried to stay in timing with Mr. Moyne for the final overhead lift off stage, but her plié was late.

"Breathe in when I pick you up," Mr. Moyne whispered to her. But it was over.

Miss Sutton excused Sara.

"Pretty good," Erin smiled at her. But Sara knew it hadn't been good enough.

When Erin was called to try it, she danced very well, but appeared to be a bit small for the part. The last intermediates to compete for the part were Lin Tan, a precise wisp of a dancer, and Kathy Jacobs, a sturdy and solid dancer from what Sara could see. While Miss Sutton and Madame compared notes, deciding who would get the solos, Sara sat under the barre amazed at how much had been accomplished at the first rehearsal. She glanced at the posters and hoped she could dance well enough to uphold the ballet's tradition.

"All right dancers," Miss Sutton said. "If I call your name, step forward." She read the names of several girls, and Robin smiled and went to the center of the room with them. "These are your soloists," Miss Sutton announced. Robin had won the little part with Mr. Moyne. All the larger roles were awarded to seniors. Sara looked at Erin.

"Wow," Erin said. "Robin got that part with Mr. Moyne."

"She was good," Sara admitted. She felt relieved and disappointed at the same time. I'm happy to just be in this at all, she thought. Maybe next year I'll be that good too. But what was it worth to be good enough for a solo next year if she wouldn't be here?

Miss Sutton wasn't finished. "The following girls will understudy the soloists," she said, calling a few seniors. But then Kathy Jacobs was called to understudy a senior, and Sara gasped when she heard her own name called as understudy to Robin. "Please step behind your soloist, girls."

Sara looked at Erin in surprise, and ran to the center of the room to stand behind Robin. Wow, she thought. How quickly things can change. Robin turned and stared at Sara over her shoulder. I'll get her part if anything happens, Sara thought. But what could happen?

CHAPTER TWELVE

"The Red Tin"

Sara and Erin headed for the drinking fountain the minute modern class ended. "I feel like I'm never going to catch on in there," Sara complained. She felt exhausted from the heat and from having to work so hard. "It isn't like ballet, where you know what exercise is coming next at the barre and most of the movements center-floor are at least familiar." She wiped her face with her hand and watched cold water spring into the air as Erin drank from the fountain. "And I don't know if I'll ever be able throw myself off-center or do those contractions."

Erin finished and moved out of the way. Sara was still trying to catch her breath in the stifling air. The dance building windows were open, but only hot air seemed to blow in. Whoever built the dance studio in the northern woods must have thought it would be cool all the time. What a joke. She let the water fill her entire mouth before drinking it down.

"I'll tell you one thing," Erin said. "Miss Casey's classes are a lot harder than the modern classes I take at home."

Sara let the cold fountain water soak a few paper towels, and then she put one on her forehead. "Really?" She moved

51

away from the fountain to let the girl behind her step ahead, and then she stuck one of the wet towels on Erin's forehead.

"Really," Erin laughed, grabbing a wet towel from Sara's hand and slapping it onto Sara's cheek.

"Really!" Sara giggled, sticking a towel on Erin's neck.

"OK, you two!" Miss Casey called. But she was smiling.

"The heat's got us," Erin laughed as Sara grabbed her arm and they headed down the stairs.

Sara sat in the locker room staring at her bare feet. "My feet are half ballet and half modern," she told Erin. "Band-Aids on my blisters from pointe, and tape on my sore spots from modern."

"Hurry," Erin said, looking at the clock. "I'm starving, and I want to go back to the cabin and check our mail before dinner." They had rehearsal that night, so if they didn't check for mail now, they wouldn't get it until after nine o'clock.

Sara got up and peeled off her leotard and tights, letting them land around her feet. The modern dance class seemed to be part of the heap on the floor. But Sara knew that even if it was behind her for today, this was only Tuesday, and tomorrow afternoon she'd be in modern class again. And it would be that way every day for the rest of the summer. She stared at the schedule she had taped to the inside of her locker and felt trapped. She was floundering in modern when she needed to be one of the best dancers in there if she was going to get a scholarship. They were going to have to squeeze in extra practices on their own. "I have a plan," she told Erin.

"Tell me on the way to the cabin…. Please?" Erin let her body slide down the doorframe, pretending to pass out. Sara laughed.

As they hurried down the path, Sara got Erin to agree to help her with modern dance on their breaks and on weekends. And Sara would help Erin with tap. Maybe there was hope. Sara opened the screen door and saw a letter and a package on her bunk. The letter was from Jen Hutchins, her best friend at school. "Cool!" she said, staring at Jen's artistic handwriting.

"Open the package first!" Erin coaxed. Sara put the letter down and tore off the brown paper to find a shiny red tin. She pulled the lid off and the delicious smell of homemade chocolate chip cookies filled the air. A note from her mom fell out.

"All *right*!" Erin grinned. They gobbled a cookie.

"Let's put them under my bed behind our ballet shoe boxes," Erin said.

"OK," Sara said. "We'll be the secret Red Tin Club!"

The dinner bell clanged as Erin came out from under her bed. Sara stuck her letter from Jen and the note from her mom under her pillow, and they ran to dinner.

When they returned from rehearsal that night, Sara was hungry again and wished she could have one of the cookies from the tin. But Becky and Danielle were there, and she figured she didn't need any more calories anyway. She pulled her shoes off, threw them over by the door, and climbed onto her bunk. She pulled the letters from her mom and Jen from under the pillow and read the note from her mom first.

"My mom can't come to *Sylphides* because she has a computer conference that weekend," Sara told Erin. "She tried to get out of it, but she's the systems trainer where she works, so she has to go." Sara felt disappointed. She was proud of her mom, but there always seemed to be some things Sara had to do alone.

"What about your dad? Erin asked.

"That will never happen," Sara said. She hadn't seen him since Christmas.

"Well, *my* parents say they can't come because it's too far away from New York for a weekend trip," Erin said. "Anyway, my dad sees patients on Saturdays." She waved her letter toward Sara. "Maybe if we had solos or something they'd come."

"Yeah, it isn't like we're the stars or anything." She opened the letter from Jen and felt immediately better. It was written with blue, yellow, and red ink so the letter looked like a piece of art. And she had drawn dancers up and down the margins! Wow, Sara thought, picturing all the posters Jen had made and strung across the halls at school.

"Hey, party girls!" Robin hollered through the door. She and Hillary came in with green flyers.

"We're invited to the boys camp!" Hillary announced. "This Saturday!"

She tacked a flyer on the bulletin board over the chest of drawers. Sara read it:

Camp Lakewood Intermediates! Come to a hot dog roast and DJ party at Camp Will-O-Green Saturday, July 23 at 6 p.m.

Saturday! Just four days away, Sara thought.

"Cool!" Danielle smiled.

"Do we get to go alone?" Becky asked.

"Right," Robin said. "Like they're going to let us go over there at night by ourselves."

"Well, the boys' counselors will be there," Danielle reasoned.

"Believe me," Robin said. "Mary will go with us."

"I think it's going to be fun," Erin said. She jumped up and scratched her poison ivy.

"I've got to get these clothes off and put medicine on these blisters."

"How did you get that poison ivy?" Robin asked. "You must have gone off-limits—they spray everything on the main grounds."

Erin looked at Sara.

"I don't know," Erin said. "Just off one of the paths. I guess they must have missed some." She went into the bathroom.

Robin stared at Sara. "Where did she get that poison ivy?"

"Lights out!" Mary called through their door.

"Lights out!" Sara repeated as she pulled the light chain overhead.

CHAPTER THIRTEEN

"Saturday's Sorrows"

S aturday morning Sara woke shivering. She pulled her bedroll and extra blanket up around her ears and wondered how the weather could change so fast. She thought if she looked out the window she might see the ground covered with snow. They didn't have rehearsal for a while, so she could just stay in bed under the covers. But oatmeal and hot chocolate sounded good.

"Shower's all yours," Erin whispered from across the room.

When it was time for rehearsal, they ran to the dance building to find everyone dressed in big pants and sweaters. Sara put her knit body suit over her leotard, a sweatshirt over that, and socks over her pointe shoes. She looked at Erin who was drowning in big pants and a floppy sweater. They wouldn't take a glamour award, but dancers' muscles had to be warm. "Your body is your instrument," Sara could hear Miss Abbey saying.

She sat on the floor and began stretching, but she was thinking about the party that would begin in just a few hours. Then she remembered that in just one week she'd be up on the stage with lights shining on her and the San Francisco Ballet watching. She sure didn't feel ready. They hadn't even learned the last steps yet. Today, she told herself, she would try not to follow anyone else in the mirror. There would be no mirror on stage—just the black void that was the audience.

During the run-through practice Sara listened carefully to the music and tried to sense the other dancers so she could help the group move as a unit. When Robin ran out for her little part with Mr. Moyne, Sara watched every detail and did the movements in her mind.

The second time through, she had a moment of panic when Miss Sutton asked the understudies to dance the solos. She hadn't actually danced the part except at that first rehearsal when she'd felt so awkward, and Robin and Mr. Moyne had it down beautifully now. But suddenly, there she was, running out to Mr. Moyne while Robin's eyes followed her every move. She did the waltz steps as softly as she could, then felt Mr. Moyne's hands on her waist at just the right moment. He lifted her high overhead, but she felt constricted by her body sweater and couldn't stretch her legs enough. It was less than spectacular. For the second lift, she couldn't seem to get into her plié soon enough to give herself a boost, so Mr. Moyne just lifted her off the floor like a doll. When she got to the highest point overhead, Madame said, "Breathe in, Sara!" But it all happened too quickly.

Great, she thought, taking her place in the group again. Robin was still staring at her from across the room like Sara was trying to steal her part or something. But Sara was glad that Robin would be the one doing it for real.

An hour into rehearsal, they were called in alphabetical order to the lower level for costume fittings. When it was her turn, Sara was amazed. The costume room was filled with rows of gauzy gowns and fluffy skirts hanging brilliantly before her eyes. Red netting, yellow lace, blue ribbons, pink taffeta, and silver sequins filled the space. It was like every fairy tale coming to life at once. She spotted the white sylph costumes hanging together near the fitting room. Their elegance took her breath. Layer upon layer of long white skirt netting seemed to hold the dresses lightly together in the air while the satin tops with their tiny ribbon straps were soft and delicate.

"Up here, please," the seamstress smiled, a measuring tape dangling around her neck. Sara climbed up onto the fitting platform while the seamstress went through the costumes until she found the one she wanted. Sara felt the tickle of stiff netting on her face as the costume fell over her head and body. When she opened her eyes and looked into the mirror, instead of a beautiful fairy she saw a disheveled girl. The skirt fell all the way to her toes. The straps fell off her shoulders. The top gaped out to the sides with room for another person. The seamstress zipped up the back and pulled it tighter, but there wasn't much improvement. The costumes seemed intended for senior dancers.

"We'll just take in the sides, hike up the straps, and hem the skirt," the seamstress said brightly. "It'll be fine, you'll see." But Sara's heart had fallen as low as the hem of the skirt.

Then Robin's face appeared in the mirror. "It's the incredible shrinking ballerina," she laughed to the senior girl next to her as though Sara should think it was funny. Thanks a lot, Sara thought, wishing her name began with an A. If it did, she'd be out of here by now, and probably with the right costume.

"There I was in that huge costume," she told Erin after rehearsal, "when Robin shows up." They were hurrying back to the cabin, so they'd have time to figure out what to wear to the party.

Erin looked at her watch. "It's already five-thirty, and we're supposed to leave at six," she said. "My feet hurt, and I'm starving."

"So then she says," Sara continued, trying to keep up, " 'Oh, look! The incredible shrinking ballerina'."

"What did you say?" Erin asked, walking ahead of Sara again.

"Nothing. I couldn't think of anything."

"Well, don't worry about it. Robin can be annoying." Erin looked at her watch again.

But Sara was beginning to think of Robin as more than an annoyance. It was like Robin was an obstacle in Sara's path, but Robin acted like Sara was the obstacle in *her* path. It was true, Sara thought, that she seemed to be in Robin's way ever since class placement auditions, or was always looking stupid in front of her, or was getting her boyfriend's arms around her, or almost getting Robin's solo.

They went in the cabin and found Hillary ready in jeans and a red flannel shirt, and Danielle and Becky in Lakewood sweatshirts. Sara tried to think of what she could wear with her jeans to be warm and still look good. She pulled her hair out of the rehearsal bun letting the thick brown waves fall around her shoulders. Robin came in, slamming the door, as usual. Sara was still angry about Robin's comment, but this wasn't the time to say something. When Sara came out of the bathroom after her shower, Danielle and Becky had gone, and Robin was putting make-up on Hillary to match her own. The mascara, blush, and red lipstick looked overdone to Sara. "You're not going to perform, you guys," Sara told them. "You don't need stage make-up." It just slipped out.

"You don't need to tell us what to do," Hillary said, checking herself out in the mirror. "And we're not *guys*."

"It's a party," Robin said.

Sara decided not to say anything else. Maybe I'm jealous or something, she thought, picturing Robin dancing effortlessly with Mr. Moyne. She put her jeans on and looked for her shoes.

"Do you want to wear this, Sara?" Erin held a beautiful dark purple sweater with blue designs.

"Do you mean it? Don't you want to wear it?" She took it from Erin.

"No. I'm going to wear my black jeans and jacket," Erin said, holding the dark jacket against her white hair.

"Let's go," Robin said to Hillary. "See you later, kids!" she called to Sara and Erin as she shut the door.

"Kids!" Sara exclaimed.

"I know," Erin said. "Kids—like we're years younger than they are!"

"We're not *guys,*" Sara said, imitating Hillary. Then she burst out laughing, and so did Erin. She found her navy turtleneck, put it on, then pulled Erin's sweater over it. She brushed her hair and put on a touch of lipstick. She liked the way she looked except she missed wearing her locket. She was going to have to find the courage to ask Madame for it. They went out the door just as Mary called "Let's go!"

CHAPTER FOURTEEN

"Saturday Night"

They took a narrow lane through thick trees to Camp Will-O-Green that was on the side of the lake opposite the secret path. Chipmunks scurried in front of them, and Sara kept her eyes open for snakes. "Watch out for poison ivy," Erin reminded her.

They entered the grounds under a big wooden "Camp Will-O-Green" sign. Sara felt like she was arriving in a strange land. "There they are," she told Erin, spotting some boys and separating them into "yes" and "no" categories.

"OK," Mary shouted. "We'll meet back here under this sign at *exactly* ten o'clock. Have a good time and stay on the boys' grounds. Understood?" Everyone nodded. She led them forward to the bonfire. Sara saw long tables of relishes, rolls, potato chips, and big buckets of ice and soda. The counselors tended several smoking barbeque grills along the front of the dining hall, but the hamburgers weren't ready to eat. The boys were jostling around, and poking at the bonfire.

"Let's check out their beach," Erin said.

Sara was curious to see it up close. She followed Erin along the sand and looked at the line of boats tied to the dock. Brightly colored sailboats rocked gently in the water, their sails put away for the evening. The green and white one she had seen the boy cleaning had the name "Will-O-Way" painted on the stern. Next to the sailboats, the big wooden rowboats were old-fashioned looking. "I'll bet you can get four guys in one of these," Sara said, staring at the varnished seats.

"Or two guys and two girls," a deep voice said behind her.

Sara turned to see a handsome dark-haired boy smiling down at her. "Hi," he said. "I'm Hank. This is Paul." Paul's hair was as blond as Hank's was dark.

"Hi," Sara answered. He was the one she had seen cleaning the boat. "I'm Sara. This is Erin."

"Hi," Erin said. "Wow—our beach and raft sure look small from here." She pointed across the lake where Sara could see miniature girls coming out of a toy-like dining hall.

"Yeah, I know. We must look small from your side too," Hank grinned. "Which is why it's a good thing we're both on the same side for a change—we all look normal!" Sara noticed his dark blue eyes and a dimple in his chin when he laughed.

"Hey, Hank! Paul!" another boy yelled from the lawn above. "Mr. Field's looking for you!"

Hank waved in response. "We have to go help out up there. I'll see you later," he promised, looking back at Sara as he and Paul took off up the hill.

Sara picked up a stone and skipped it on the surface of the lake. "Wow!" she said. "Six skips!"

"Must mean good things for you," Erin smiled.

Sara picked up another stone and skimmed it across the water. "Oh, that's probably the last I'll see of Hank," she said. But this time Sara counted seven lucky rings.

"We know where the horses are!" Becky exclaimed, running up to Sara and Erin with Danielle close behind. She pointed toward an area where a path beyond the cabins disappeared into the woods.

"But is it on the grounds?" Sara asked, looking for a horse barn or stable.

"She likes horses more than boys," Danielle teased.

"Horses are cool," Becky said. "And better looking than most of the boys I know in Wisconsin."

"But have you seen the boys here?" Erin asked. "Will-O-Green seems to have more than the average number of cute guys per pine tree."

Sara pictured Hank's smile. Then the dinner bell rang and she took off with the rest of the crowd into the excitement of the evening.

Before Sara knew it, it seemed, Mary was under the "Camp Will-O-Green" sign, as promised, at exactly ten o'clock. She moved the beams of a big flashlight around, and asked if everybody was there as she began to count them. "No," Hillary said. "Robin's not here."

"Yes, I am," Robin's voice called to them just before she appeared in the stream of Mary's light. Mary moved the flashlight off Robin's face, and began her count again. Sara was close enough to hear Robin murmur "Thanks a lot" to Hillary.

When Mary was satisfied that everyone was accounted for, she led them onto the path to their cabins. Sara looked over her shoulder to get a final glimpse of the low-burning fire. There was so much to tell Erin, but she'd wait until they were alone. She held her new memories in silence as she wound her way around the lake surrounded by giggling girls trying to avoid low hanging tree branches. Suddenly a high-pitched scream filled the dark woods. Sara froze and felt her neck stiffen as Erin grabbed her arm. Mary stopped and flashed her light on them.

"Hillary!" Robin shouted. "You really scared us!"

"Well, that branch felt just like a man's arm to me!" Hillary said.

"Well, your head feels just like mush to us!" somebody in the group said too quietly for Mary to hear. Everyone laughed, and Sara felt her heart slow. Erin let go of her sleeve.

"That's enough," Mary scolded. "Let's go. Try to stay in the middle of the road." Sara felt how dark it was, how thick the forest. She looked up at the sky and saw a trace of moon through heavy black clouds, and stayed close to Erin for the rest of the walk home.

But at midnight Hillary did it again. Her scream pierced the cabin. Becky switched on the light from her top bunk. "What!?" she demanded. Sara blinked at Hillary in the bright light. Erin sat up in her bunk under Hillary and rubbed her eyes. Danielle stared.

"I swear!" Hillary said. "I saw a man this time! I heard a noise, so I peeked through the curtain, and there he was, walking away into the woods!" She sat perched in her bunk looking into everyone's disbelieving faces. "I swear!"

Robin groaned and lay back down. "Hillary, go to sleep," she told her, unconvinced. "I have rehearsal tomorrow."

Danielle got up, climbed into Erin's bunk, opened the curtain, and looked out. "Turn off the light," she told Becky. A few seconds after the light had gone out, Danielle said, "I don't see anything." She went back to bed.

Sara lay back on her pillow. It had probably been a branch hitting Hillary's window, she thought, remembering the crash against her own window the first week of camp. She turned over and felt for her flashlight. Then she remembered there was no tree next to Hillary's window. She quietly turned back and parted the curtains next to her head. She looked past the pine tree and let her eyes adjust to the distance. She scanned the path to her right that led to the dining hall but saw nothing. She looked straight ahead and was about to let the curtains fall shut when she looked to her left where the path led to the lookout bench. A tiny white light, like a flashlight bobbing, seemed to disappear into the trees. She looked harder, straining to see, but lost it. She blinked and looked again, but the light was gone.

She closed the curtains. Wow, she thought, your imagination sure can play tricks on you. It was probably just a star. But as she sunk again into her bedroll, she remembered there were no stars out that night.

CHAPTER FIFTEEN

"The Secret Cabin"

S unday morning, Sara and Erin headed down to the beach. Sara would let Erin speak first. "I had a great time with Paul," Erin began. "He showed me the Will-O-Way after you and Hank went in to dance. They're almost fifteen, you know," she said.

"We're almost fourteen," Sara said. There wasn't much movement across the lake except for a couple of boys dismantling the tables. "You two looked great dancing together," she told Erin.

"Well," Erin said to Sara, bounding down the stairs that led to the sand. "Tell me everything! What happened with you and Hank? Where did you guys go for so long? Paul and I were about to go looking for you."

"Hank wanted to show me the horses," Sara said.

Erin sat on one of the steps and Sara joined her. "He took me down that path that Becky and Danielle had pointed out to us."

Erin looked surprised. "Wasn't that off-limits? How far into the woods was it?"

"I'm still not exactly sure where we were," Sara said. "It was so dark. But I remembered that Becky and Danielle had been there, so I assumed it would be OK."

"But Becky and Danielle didn't actually go there," Erin told her. "Someone told them about it, that's all."

Sara felt betrayed. "Really? Are you sure?"

Erin was sure. "Yes. I asked them about it when I couldn't find you."

"They don't know I went to the horse barn, do they?"

"No," Erin assured her. "And I'm sure they couldn't care less. So what happened?"

"We went into the barn," Sara began carefully, remembering the smell of leather and horse dung, the sound of the horses neighing. "There was a bit of light coming through a slatted door, so I could see some of the horses. Hank put his arm around me, then I heard a noise and thought I saw eyes staring at us from the slats in the door. I got scared and found my way out, but I couldn't find the path in the dark. I was just running, trying to get back to the bonfire. I was heading the wrong way and ran into a ramshackled old cabin."

"Was anybody there?" Erin asked.

"I'm not sure. It was dark inside. Hank was right behind me and got us back to the path to the boys camp. I would have been lost in the woods forever!"

Erin's eyes opened wide. "Sara. Let's go back there and try to find the cabin. We don't have rehearsal until two o'clock."

"Why?" Sara felt frightened even though it was daylight.

"Wouldn't it be cool to have a place to go? A secret place in the woods where no one could find us?"

"But I have no idea where I was. We could get really lost out there."

"Come on, Sara," Erin insisted. "We have plenty of time. Think of it—our own secret cabin."

They checked out a rowboat and took it to the shore where they figured the path to the boys camp met the stream. Hopping out, they pulled the boat in among the trees as far as they could. "Look!" Sara whispered. "There's the path." They followed it to the stream and knew the boys camp was up to the right, and the horse barn behind it several yards into the woods.

"If we find the horse barn, can you get to the old cabin?" Erin asked.

"Follow me," Sara said, heading up the path. She saw the camp in the clearing to her right, then looked up at the trees to locate the horse barn. "There!" she pointed. Erin followed as Sara scrambled deeper into the woods. They saw the barn, but stopped before getting close enough to be seen.

"OK, which way did you run from the barn last night?" Erin asked.

"That way," Sara pointed, waving Erin on. She went around the back of the barn, then took off through the trees. When she stopped, she knew she was lost.

"Where's the cabin?" Erin asked.

Sara shrugged. "I don't even know which way the barn is now." The sun was getting higher in the sky. She worried they wouldn't find their way back, that Mary would find their abandoned rowboat down in the trees long after rehearsal ended. Erin found an old tree stump to sit on and looked around. In the silence, Sara thought she heard a chopping sound. Erin stood and they listened carefully, but everything was still. There was no clue to get them back to the boat. Sara cupped her hands near her mouth ready to call out for help when she saw the deer. It turned, and they decided to follow it through the trees. But they lost it when it took off quickly over a tiny branch of the stream. Sara jumped over the trickle of water and tried to figure out which way the deer had gone.

She looked upstream of the rivulet of water, then downstream. She thought she saw brown among the green trees upstream, but doubted her senses. It was too dark to be the deer and it wasn't moving. They took several steps toward it. "It's the cabin!" Sara whispered.

It looked completely abandoned with torn screens, a broken door, loose roof shingles, and missing cement between the logs. The girls approached it cautiously. When they were sure no one was around, they pressed their faces against the windows. There was a single bed in the room, one chair at an old table, a rusty skillet hanging on the wall. She turned the knob on the old wood door to no avail. She pushed it with her shoulder and walked through cobwebs.

"Cool," Erin said looking over the kitchen. "This is really cool."

"Kind of dirty," Sara said looking at the yellowed linoleum floor strewn with acorns.

"Who cares?" Erin said. She sat down on the bed and dust rose up in the streak of sunlight coming in the window.

"We won't even remember how to get here," Sara said. "Besides, it might be off-limits."

"No one knows about it. No one would ever know we were here," Erin said. She got up and started tap dancing in the middle of the room. "See? We could practice here."

Sara told herself it might be OK to use the cabin for practice. "Red tin promise that we won't tell anyone else about this cabin?"

"Red tin promise!" Erin said, slapping Sara's upheld hand. They closed the door tightly behind them and set out to find their way back.

Sara remembered the little deer that led them to the water. They found the rivulet and followed it until it turned into the larger stream, traversed the old plank connecting the boys camp grounds to the girls' side, and quickly found the boat they'd left in the trees.

CHAPTER SIXTEEN

"Turn of Events"

Practices were long and hard in the days before Friday night's dress rehearsal. On Sunday they finished learning the movements to *Les Sylphides*, and on Wednesday evening they did the ballet facing the wall instead of the mirrors. Sara felt disoriented a couple of times, not being able to see all the other dancers. She was hoping for a smoother runthrough tonight, Thursday, the last full rehearsal in the studio. She sat in the locker room next to Erin and put on her pointe shoes. Then she stood on them to test the sore spot she had covered with a Band-Aid.

"Want to go to our cabin tomorrow?" Erin whispered.

"Oh, right," Sara said sarcastically. "We'll go in the time off Miss Sutton's sure to give us the day before a performance."

"Lunch hour."

"Skip lunch?" Sara was always hungry.

Erin shut her locker door. "We have to do *something* besides rehearse. I'm going cuckoo," she whispered as loud as she dared. "Let's at least grab a power bar for lunch, and take a boat out to see Paul and Hank. We'll just row out to the middle, drop anchor, and wave them out to join us."

It didn't sound like too risky a plan to Sara. "Let's see how tired we are after tap," she said.

But Erin looked disappointed. "Oh, come on, Sara."

"I guess so." But inside Sara felt a pendulum swinging back and forth between a dance scholarship and disaster. "Next week," she told Erin, "we'll start our private practices. We can start Monday."

"Say good-bye to swimming," Erin sighed.

Robin heard Erin and butted in. "Like you're such good swimmers, anyway," she said, looking at Sara.

Like I'd fake drowning to get David to rescue me, Sara thought. "I'll get better," she said.

At least rehearsal was good. Sara was beginning to feel confident that she would perform well enough to stay on pointe through the long bourrées at the beginning, that she would blend into the group with the seniors. Now if her costume fit, everything would be fine. She was worried, of course, about messing up in front of the San Francisco Ballet dancers, but that was a different kind of worrying—it had an excitement about it that could even make you dance better.

At the end of class Miss Sutton announced that the professional ballet company would perform *Swan Lake* for them on Sunday—one of the most beautiful and romantic ballets ever created. When the velvet curtains open on *Swan Lake*, Sara smiled in excitement, *Les Sylphides* would be safely behind her.

"We'll have a run-through of *Sylphides* tomorrow right after lunch, with a final costume-fitting. You'll have your afternoon classes, then you are to be at the theater at six o'clock sharp for a full dress rehearsal." With that, Miss Sutton released

all of them but the senior soloists. Erin winced at the tough
schedule.

"Looks like we'll be eating regular lunch tomorrow," Sara
said, "instead of doing the power bar in a boat." Erin agreed.
Everything will be fine, Sara thought. All she needed was one
more good rehearsal and she'd be ready for the stage.

She fell asleep easily that night, imagining her fluffy white
costume fitting perfectly. She was deep in sleep when Mary
checked for lights-out at ten. But then came a turn of events.
Sara woke in the darkness to Hillary's urgent whispers. "Sara!
Sara! I saw that man again!" She sat up and looked around.
It was five after eleven. Mary would be by for bed-check at
eleven-thirty.

"Sara, I mean it! Get up! I can't turn the light on—nobody
will believe me!"

Sara was awake enough now to realize that her sleep had
been interrupted on the night before dress rehearsal. She told
Hillary to go back to bed, then opened her window curtain
to check for a man or a light. There was nothing there, so she
whispered it again. "Go back to bed, Hillary." But Hillary
stood glued to her spot. "You're going to wake everybody up!"
Sara warned.

"But look!" Hillary said. "Erin's gone!" She pulled back the
bedroll lying like a ghost over a strange lump.

Sara quickly tiptoed over to the bunk. The rough wool of
a blanket met her fingers instead of Erin's skin. She pulled her
hand back and stood stiffly in her nightgown and cold feet.
What a cheap old trick, she thought.

"There really is a man out there!" Hillary whispered.

Sara thought fast. Why would Hillary lie when she had no
audience this time?

Erin wanted to go out on the lake to meet the boys tomorrow. Would she have gone out to meet Paul tonight? She remembered how she thought she'd seen a flashlight bobbing in the woods the last time Hillary had screamed in the night. Maybe it was real. She had to find Erin. "Go back to bed!" she ordered Hillary. "Don't wake up anybody else!"

Hillary jumped onto her bunk. "Are you going out there?" she whispered.

Sara stepped barefoot into her shoes, grabbed the flashlight from under her pillow, and turned to Hillary. "Just be *quiet*!" she told her. "If you tell anybody..."

Danielle mumbled and turned in her sleep. Sara turned the doorknob quietly, but when she pulled the old door toward her, it squeaked. She left it open and ran away from the cabin. She'd have to get Erin and be back before Mary's bed-check. But which way should she go? The woods scared her. She'd check the beach.

The torches at the lake were out and the moon sunk behind a cloud. There was nothing to guide her, but she couldn't turn on the flashlight yet—somebody might see it from a cabin window. Her heart pounded as her feet slapped the ground, her shoelaces and nightgown flying. She crouched behind the low stone wall dividing the dining hall lawn from the beach steps. The moon came out a bit, and she looked around but saw nothing. She ran her hand against the bumpy stones looking for the opening to the stairs. When she found it, she raced down the steps, looking one way, then the other. But it was too dark to see anything that might be hidden in the trees along either side. She got to the sand, felt it spray into her loose shoes, and heard the wind lapping the water against the shore.

She could sweep the entire beach with the flashlight, but decided to find the dock before turning it on. Maybe Paul had rowed over and tied up. Her heart raced, and she felt the chill air blow through her nightgown as she moved toward the dock. Sand squeaked under her shoes as she made her way along the wide planks, the water getting blacker and deeper beneath her. "Erin," she whispered. She clicked on the flashlight, but saw no one. She turned off the light and looked across the water to the boys camp. A few lights twinkled through the trees. If Paul hadn't come across the lake, there was another route—the secret path!

She turned on the flashlight long enough to find the trail to the lookout bench, then darted uphill to find the stand of tall pines. But the moon was behind the clouds, and she couldn't find the path. Everything looked the same: swaying trees, snarly fern, and tangled brush everywhere. "Erin!" she called into the forest. Suddenly, the moon came out. Sara looked up and saw the cluster of pines at the beginning of the path. She charged into the thick brush and turned on the flashlight. Its ray bounced off the green fern as she twisted with the path toward the other side of the lake.

She ran fast, feeling the trail slope. The air grew colder and held the smell of mint. She felt her shoes sink into mucky earth she knew was as black as the night, and she heard the bubbling of the stream. She thought of the snake she saw the last time she was there and stopped. She ran to her right, trying to find the old plank downstream. If she had to cross it and go off-limits to the boys' side to find Erin, she would. She found the old board and quickly jumped on, trying to clear the thinnest section.

The next thing she knew, Robin and David were in the glow of her flashlight at the end of the plank. Robin screamed and David took off into the woods. Sara froze. Robin tried to shield her eyes from the light and scurried across the plank toward Sara. As Robin got near, Sara remembered the danger of the thin wood. She jumped onto the ground, but it was too late. The board cracked under their weight, and Robin cried out as her right foot fell through the jagged wood into the water.

"Robin," Sara said, trying to help her up.

Robin quickly pulled her foot out, pushed past Sara, and limped up the path in pain.

Sara ran to her. "Robin," she said again.

"Leave me alone," Robin sobbed.

Sara watched Robin make her way through the trees and fern. She felt a lump in her throat and began to cry. Then she told herself that would do no good. She had to find Erin. There was only one place left to try. She made her way up the hill through the thicket, staying well behind Robin. When she saw Robin turn left toward the cabins, she took the right fork to the lookout bench. As she got close, she turned off her flashlight and ducked behind a tree. But she peered out to see a completely empty bench. She was sure time was up. She'd have to get back. "Erin!" she called half-heartedly. As she said it, a twig snapped behind her and she took off like a racehorse.

The heavy door squeaked as she opened it. She shook off her mucky shoes and tiptoed around the bunks. Hillary, Becky, and Danielle were sleeping like bears in winter. Robin huddled under her covers, and there was Erin—asleep in her bed like she'd never left! Suddenly there were footsteps on the porch. She clambered onto her bunk, pulled up her bedroll, turned toward the wall, and closed her eyes. The door opened and a flashlight beam swept the room. "Bed-check," Mary whispered.

CHAPTER SEVENTEEN

"Unravelings"

Sara woke to find Erin braiding her hair for their nine o'clock ballet class like nothing had happened. Hillary's bunk was empty. Danielle and Becky were still asleep. She hung her head over her bunk to see that Robin was gone too. Sara's groggy head flooded with everything she had to do that day: ballet, tap, lunch, costume-fitting, *Les Sylphides* rehearsal, modern, folk, dinner, dress rehearsal. She was exhausted from last night's events and wanted another two hours of sleep. But there was only one hour before Madame's ballet class, and she was desperate to talk to Erin.

"Erin," Sara whispered. "Where are Robin and Hillary?"

Erin turned and looked at Sara with a calmness that belied the truth of her zany adventure. "I don't know," she said. "They were gone when I woke up."

"Hurry up," she told Erin. "I have to talk to you." She jumped out of bed, got dressed, grabbed her dance bag, and they were out the door.

Over breakfast Sara told Erin every detail of what had happened the night before. Erin's mouth nearly spilled her scrambled eggs. "You mean, you went wandering in the woods in the dead of night looking for me?" she asked incredulously. "Are you crazy?"

"What do you mean, am *I* crazy?" Sara said. "Where were you? What were you doing out there after lights-out?"

"Oh, I only met Paul at the lookout bench for a minute. I got back by bed-check," Erin said. "Everyone was sound asleep when I left."

"Apparently Robin wasn't. When Hillary woke me up I was so scared about you that I didn't even notice Robin wasn't in her bunk. I just took off. But it figures, because Hillary would have told Robin about seeing the man instead of me if Robin had been there." Sara looked at Erin. She must have just missed her at the lookout bench. "Why didn't you tell me you were going to do that?"

"I didn't know that I would actually do it until the last minute," Erin said. "After everybody fell asleep it seemed like it would be easy to do it and get back before bed-check. I thought if you didn't know about it, you wouldn't get into trouble."

"Well, *that* plan didn't work," Sara said. "If Robin and Hillary tell Mary, I'm probably in bigger trouble than you are."

"But if they tell, then you can say that you saw Robin out there with David," Erin said.

"I know," Sara said wearily. "But that would be stupid."

"Talk about stupid," Erin said. "What about Hillary screaming about a crazy man?"

"Well," Sara told her. "I did see a flashlight bobbing out there the first night she pulled that after the party."

"That was Paul," Erin confessed. "He came over after the party and slipped a note under the cabin door for me. I put it in the red tin."

"The red tin? I didn't see any note in there," Sara said.

"I hid it under the foil at the bottom," Erin explained.

"What did it say?" Sara asked, wondering how Erin could have left her out of so much.

"That he had a great time with me at the party, and that he wanted me to meet him at the bench last night," Erin said.

Sara thought of something. "Erin," she said. "Did Paul come to the cabin to get you last night?"

"Oh, no. He took a big enough chance coming over with the note after the party. I just met him at the bench. He was nowhere near the cabin."

"Then who did Hillary see last night?" Sara asked.

"Maybe it was Mr. Moyne," Erin said.

But Sara knew his cabin was way across camp from theirs, on the other side of the studio. And why would he be wandering around the girls' cabins? If he wanted to remain a Lakewood instructor, he wouldn't do such a thing. "No," Sara said, getting up. "I don't think so."

In the studio, Sara ran across the floor to the ballet barre just in time for pliés. It was when she turned to do them on the second side that she saw Robin limp in.

CHAPTER EIGHTEEN

"Repercussions and Rehearsals"

Robin's foot was bandaged like an injured football player's. After class she told the dancers surrounding her that she had twisted her foot falling off the cabin steps. Dress rehearsal was that night. Sara felt sick looking at the crutch against the wall.

"Girls! Girls!" Madame shouted, clapping her hands. "Robin will be fine. Change for next class now!" The dancers dispersed, but as she passed the piano, Sara felt Madame's hand on her shoulder.

"You will dance part," Madame announced, handing her the locket.

Sara nodded her understanding, but fear gripped her stomach. In the mirror, she saw Robin struggling to stand up, and she wanted to run away as fast as she could. Madame released her hand, and she and Erin went down the stairs to the locker room, letting the chattering dancers go ahead of them.

"What a mess," Sara said, holding the locket to her heart. "If I had just minded my own business, none of this would have happened."

"If *I* hadn't gone out there, *you* wouldn't have," Erin reminded her.

"Yes, but if I had just gone to the lookout bench first, I would have found you. I wouldn't have gone on the secret path and Robin wouldn't have hurt her foot."

"Well anyway," Erin said as they neared the bottom of the stairs. "You get to dance Robin's part."

If it was meant to comfort Sara, it didn't. She was terrified. "I can't do it!" she said. "I barely know it. And I look stupid doing it." Behind them, Robin was making her way down the stairs with Hillary.

"Sara, everything will be fine," Erin said. "You'll be OK dancing the part. You can do it."

Sara knew she had no choice. Anyway, she figured she'd get a chance to practice with Mr. Moyne several times before the performance. But at rehearsal Miss Sutton spent the first hour practicing the large group while Robin watched from the corner.

Just when it looked as if Miss Sutton was going to call a run-through of the entire ballet, she announced instead that the seamstress would be taking them out of class a few at a time for final fittings. Meanwhile, the large group of dancers would work with Madame and the senior soloists with Miss Sutton. I know it's a small part, Sara thought, but I absolutely have to practice it. She looked around for Mr. Moyne and, to her dismay, saw him talking to Robin. He bent over her, touched her foot, and patted her on the arm. Then he came across the room to Sara.

"Let's try the lift a couple of times," Mr. Moyne said, taking Sara's hand.

Madame nodded her approval. Erin smiled at her in excitement. In the corner farthest from Robin, Mr. Moyne coached Sara in when to plié, how to help him lift her, how to land. But it was no use. They would not have enough time to make it as good as it was with Robin. When Mr. Moyne was called for his fitting Sara rejoined the group and felt relieved not to have Robin staring at her.

Lovely, long white gowns began to grace the room as the dancers came back from their fittings, their reflections in the mirror like fairies. When Sara climbed onto the seamstress's platform, she expected the worst. But when she looked into the mirror she could hardly believe it.

"I told you!" the seamstress exclaimed.

"It's perfect." Sara smiled and rose up on her pointe shoes. The long, fragile skirt stopped gracefully just above her ankles. The straps were snug and the top—the bodice, the seamstress called it—was tight. "Thank you," she said, picturing herself high over Mr. Moyne's head, the skirt billowing in a flow of white gauze.

Madame led the group through a section of the ballet, and Sara tried to get used to moving in the tight bodice top and straps. Mr. Moyne looked like a prince in his black velvet vest over a blousy white shirt and white tights. His dark wavy hair was dampened and neatly combed. Sara was sure the costumes would create magic for their special part, holding her and Mr. Moyne majestically in the air.

But when Miss Sutton finally called a full run-through of the ballet, it was still awkward. Mr. Moyne whisked her off the floor like he'd given up on talking her through it. Apparently, there was no time left for discussion. She was simply the understudy trying to make do. Sara felt crestfallen. She did not want to be part of anything mediocre.

At dinner, Erin ate happily. "You must be so excited about dancing the part," she said. "It looks good now."

But Sara knew exactly how far from good it was. "Oh, Erin," she said. "I look awful. And don't say '*the* part'—it's Robin's part." Sara dropped her fork onto her plate and sighed. "It's my fault, and I can't get out of it and I can't make it look good." Points against a scholarship, she thought. She looked down the table at Robin and felt trapped in frustration. She got up and pushed quickly through the tables toward the door. She nearly knocked over a chair and just missed spilling a bowl of apples. She ran over the lawn and onto the path to the lookout bench rushing past trees, shrubs, and fern.

If Robin hadn't fallen through that stupid plank, everything would be going smoothly, she thought, plopping down on the bench. I would just be part of the group in the performance and everybody would say how wonderful it was that I got into the senior production. Now, she thought.... She sat on the bench and cried.

When she finally lifted her head and stared vacantly into the trees, she knew it must be time for dress rehearsal. She pictured Mr. Moyne running out center-stage to meet her and, when she wasn't there, pretending to lift an invisible girl. She saw Madame's face counting on her, heard Miss Sutton saying, *leadership, cooperation, enthusiasm, improvement.* She heard Miss Abbey telling her to try. She touched her locket, blew her nose and headed back.

CHAPTER NINETEEN

"Dress Rehearsal"

"Where were you?" Erin asked Sara in the dressing room. She had saved her a chair in front of the long make-up mirror.

"Lookout bench," Sara said. She ran to the bathroom and splashed cold water on her face. When she came out she realized she'd have to hurry. There was a frenzy of dancers around her brushing their hair, applying make-up, and taking last minute stitches in their shoe ribbons. Sara pulled everything she'd need out of her dance bag, threw her pointe shoes and tights on her chair, and tossed make-up, hairbrush, bobby-pins, and hairspray on the countertop. "Here goes," she told herself in the mirror. She peeled off her clothes and put on tights and a T-shirt. Then she pulled the brush through her hair, making a tight bun with the elastic and pins. She wound a hairnet around it and sprayed.

"Hurry," Erin said, helping Sara with her eye make-up. They threw their costumes over their heads, zipped each other up, and applied red lipstick.

"All dancers on stage please!" Miss Sutton's voice boomed over the intercom.

Sara felt tiny walking on stage in the theater. She gazed at the rows of blue velvet seats and up at the balcony wondering where the dancers from the San Francisco Ballet would sit tomorrow night. Dancers were warming up everywhere, hanging onto chairs in the wings, to the curtain ropes, or stretching against the wall.

"Over here, Sara," Erin said heading across the stage to two old chairs. As she began her warm-up, Sara saw Mr. Moyne practicing his variation in a corner of the stage. Other dancers, wrapped in sweaters, had finished their stretches and were rehearsing pirouettes. The orchestra conductor hit his baton on the music stand and gave directions to his musicians. The lighting crew and stagehands shouted at each other. Everything is so crazy, Sara thought, hoping that she'd remember the movements to the ballet in all the confusion. Before she'd had a chance to do more than her pliés, tendus, and some slow stretching, Miss Sutton's voice called out, "Opening positions, please!"

They were in the midst of the ballet before Sara realized it, pushed along by the music. The tempo seemed erratic to Sara, sometimes faster than their practice music, and other times slower. The conductor kept shouting at the musicians. Things seemed to be falling apart after all their long, careful rehearsals. "Harry, bring that ladder over here!" she heard a gruff voice shout somewhere in the darkness. "Stay in line, Karen," Miss Sutton called out from the middle of the theater. Suddenly, the stage lights came on, and Sara felt blinded in the brightness. "Take the lights down to number three!" another voice yelled.

Before Sara's eyes could adjust, it was time for her part with Mr. Moyne. She ran out to meet him, her heart jumping. Keep your head, she told herself. Think. But her foot slipped on the floor and she nearly fell. She had forgotten to step in the box of rosin before they began! She covered up her slip as best she could by cutting the little run short, and going right into the waltz steps. Mr. Moyne knew enough to go along with it, but it threw their timing off when Sara had hoped things might come together tonight. Sara waited for Madame's voice, but heard only silence in the blackness of the theater. Breathe in, she told herself, as she felt Mr. Moyne lift her the second time. It was over before she knew it, and she couldn't tell how it had gone. No one seemed to be paying attention. She ran back on stage and into the group of dancers.

The orchestra finally seemed to find a consistent tempo halfway through the ballet, and the conductor assured Miss Sutton that they would be fine the next night. After the full run-through Madame came forward and assisted Miss Sutton in having the dancers practice each part of the ballet to get the staging and spacing right. Then they practiced their bows. After the three lines of dancers came forward one at a time and bowed in unison, Miss Sutton called for Sara to come forward with Mr. Moyne for a separate little bow. Sara's heart leaped. She ran out from the line and joined Mr. Moyne downstage. But her heart fell as quickly as it had risen when she saw Robin's face staring at her from the first row. She had actually forgotten about Robin. She let Mr. Moyne take her hand as she placed one foot back and curtsied. Then she ran quickly off into the wings, feeling Robin's eyes follow her. She came back on stage and stood in line as the senior soloists practiced their bows, tired and relieved that it was nearly over for tonight.

Miss Sutton praised them. "Good rehearsal, company!" she smiled.

Company, Sara thought. For the first time, she felt a part of it. She had come out and done her best to hold her end of it together.

"We'll have a short rehearsal for the senior soloists tomorrow morning in the studio," Miss Sutton added. "Nine o'clock sharp! Everybody else get some rest tomorrow, don't sprain anything, and be in your dressing rooms by six-thirty! We'll have a thorough warm-up on stage at exactly seven-fifteen. Thank you!" The cast and crew applauded and whistled loudly. Madame glanced Sara's way but didn't say anything. Sara guessed she must have looked OK or she would have been called to the morning rehearsal. Or maybe it didn't matter—no one expected it to get any better and the other parts were more important. Anyway, after tomorrow night when the curtain closed it would be over and that would be that.

"I am *starving!*" Sara told Erin in the dressing room as she wiped off globs of make-up. After all, she hadn't eaten much dinner. Erin produced a big red apple from her bag and offered it up. Sara thought of the bowl of apples she had nearly knocked over on her way out of the dining hall. It seemed like days ago.

CHAPTER TWENTY

"The Boys Leave and The Company Arrives"

In the morning Sara stared up at the rafters above her bunk. She closed her eyes and pictured herself waltzing perfectly with Mr. Moyne and rising breathlessly above him. She repeated this image again and again in her mind until she was sure she had the flow of it. Tonight was her final chance to fulfill the part.

She glanced around the room to find everyone else asleep. She looked under her bunk at Robin. In spite of all the trouble, she felt sorry for her. Then her stomach growled and she knew why she was the first one awake—she was still hungry from not eating a good dinner last night. She saw Erin stir and whispered for them to go to breakfast.

"What do you want to do today?" Sara asked when she was finally full of fruit, eggs, and toast. They had no classes or rehearsal and didn't have to be at the theater until after dinner.

"I told Paul we'd row over at ten o'clock this morning to meet them," Erin said.

"What?" Sara said. "I don't *think* so." She wanted everything to go smoothly today, and for the rest of the summer for that matter. "Why did you tell him that? We should wait until after the performance."

"Let's enact our plan to row out into the lake and drop anchor," Erin said.

Soon Sara was sitting on the front seat of a boat in her bathing suit and shorts while Erin rowed them out into the lake. She closed her eyes, tilted her head back, and felt the luscious sun. She did want to see Hank again.

"I think I see them!" Erin said. "Over there."

Paul glanced at his watch, then looked out onto the lake. He spotted them and waved. The girls waved back as the boys jumped into a boat.

"Let's put the anchor down," Sara said. She threw it over the side and watched the bubbles rise as it hit bottom. When she looked up, she saw Hank rowing toward them, his black hair tousled in the wind. Her heart felt like a summer rose opening in sunlight.

The boys dropped anchor, and jumped into the girls' boat. "Hey, what's new?" Paul asked.

"Not much except dance steps and rehearsals," Erin said.

"We got some news from your side," Paul said. "We heard Robin fell through a plank and sprained her foot." He pointed in the direction of the secret path. "Over there."

Sara cringed. She had to find out if her name had been mentioned. "But Robin said she sprained it falling off the cabin steps," she said.

"Well, David swore us to secrecy. He was bragging about being out in the woods with Robin," Hank said. "Her secret's safe with us." Little did he know it was Sara's secret too.

"Those two are destined for disaster if you ask me," Paul said.

"Why?" Erin asked.

"She and David got caught in the horse barn last year," Paul said. "They accidentally woke up old Charlie, the caretaker, and he told. I heard Robin got demoted to a lower dance class or something. David had to pull kitchen duty for the rest of camp."

Sara looked at Hank. She had been *completely* off-limits with him! The same thing might have happened to her. And those were probably old Charlie's eyes staring at her that night through the door.

"I didn't know," Hank said sincerely, looking into Sara's eyes.

So Robin was the one demoted to Class B last year! And it wasn't from bad dancing. "It would be good if you guys didn't tell anybody else," Sara said. "People could get in trouble."

"We swear on a stack of dance shoes!" Paul said.

"Case closed," Hank announced looking at his watch. "We have to get back. We're going backpacking with the horses for a few days."

"Yeah," Paul said. "They set us loose in the woods to see if we can light fires, cook food, kill bears, and find our way back."

"He's kidding about the bears," Hank smiled.

"Anyway, can you come out here next Saturday for our sailboat races?" Paul asked, throwing his arm around Hank. "Skipper here is going to take the trophy away from David."

"With your help, Salty," Hank said.

"Skipper?" Sara teased.

"Salty?" Erin grinned.

"The crew of the Will-O-Way at your service!" Paul jumped into their boat and Hank followed. They pulled up anchor.

"We'll ask," Sara promised.

"Have fun getting lost in the woods," Erin said.

"Yeah," Sara laughed. "Watch out for those bears." Hank smiled at her, and the rose that was her heart opened completely.

Back in the cabin Sara ripped open a mailing envelope from Jen. This time when she wrote about girls, she wrote in silver, like the moon. When she wrote about boys, she used gold, like the sun. From her news, it didn't sound like Sara was missing much. But the letter made her remember other summers when she and Jen had just hung out, read books, and gone shopping. For a second she wished for that again, but then she couldn't imagine not dancing every day. She felt excited to be in the Pavlova cabin that very minute, the performance just ahead of her.

A long banner fell out of the envelope. "Look!" she said to Erin, unfurling the paper. *BREAK A LEG IN LES SYLPHIDES*! "Break a leg" was the way dancers said good luck so they wouldn't get bad luck. Jen had drawn dancers on a stage under lights, and had named two of them "Sara" and "Erin".

"Cool!" Erin smiled. "Let's put it on the wall." They took the tacks out of the old poster for the boys' party, and hung the banner on the big wall against the bathroom. Sara walked backward to her bunk staring at it. Wow, she thought. This really makes the whole thing real! She checked the time in a countdown to the performance. It was already eleven-thirty.

On the way to lunch, they ran into Danielle and Becky. "The San Francisco Ballet dancers are in the big studio! Let's go!" They all took off running, but when they got to the dance building, they found a note on the door that said *CLOSED REHEARSAL*. They ran around back and found a cluster of girls peering into the tall windows. Sara couldn't believe what she saw. The dancers legs were perfectly turned-out, their feet arched with high insteps, their muscles rippled in developed control and precise tension and release. She watched carefully as all the finely tuned feet in worn ballet slippers brushed the floor in unison.

"Look at those extensions!" Sara said as the dancers slowly raised their legs high to the side. "Their legs are way over their heads!" Sara wondered if she'd ever be that good. They watched until the dancers left the barre and moved center-floor. They would miss lunch if they stayed longer. It was an option Sara considered then thought better of. Not today.

After lunch Sara and Erin rushed back to the dance building to find a note on the door announcing that the company would give master classes Sunday morning for all intermediates and seniors. Wow, Sara thought. I'll have a master teacher from the San Francisco Ballet—someone I'll watch dance in *Swan Lake*! What would they think of her dancing? How would she stack up?

"Come on!" Erin said, heading for the back windows. They squeezed between the other girls to watch the company rehearsing *Swan Lake*. The women, in fluffy practice skirts, moved exactly like swans, their necks long and graceful, their arms soft and supple. Sara noticed one dancer who looked about seventeen—just a few years older than she was. Sara wondered how good she was at her age, where she'd been trained, how she got into the company. The distance to becoming a professional dancer seemed far away and very close at the same time. Each moment and every performance counted.

CHAPTER TWENTY-ONE

"The Performance"

Sara couldn't get her stomach to stop fluttering. "Hurry up," Erin told her. "Let's get right to the barre and start warming up."

"OK," Sara agreed. She knew no muscle could go unstretched tonight, and she needed a chance to get composed. She was careful to put Band-Aids on every sensitive spot on her feet, to place just the right amount of cottony lambswool in her shoes, and to sew a few stitches into her knotted shoe ribbons so they wouldn't come unraveled as she danced. As she left the dressing room, Sara held an image in her mind of the beautiful professional dancers she had watched that afternoon.

But when she reached the stage she couldn't believe what she saw. Robin was in her costume and pointe shoes doing pliés at the barre. Sara tugged at Erin's arm, pulling her back into the wings. "Look!" she whispered.

"I don't believe it," Erin said. "What does she think she's doing?" Mr. Moyne and Madame went to Robin. Sara watched as Madame asked Robin to do a slow rise on her pointe shoes and Mr. Moyne touched her injured leg. He shook his head. Madame made Robin stand flat on her shoes and got Miss Sutton. She came out onto the stage with authority and said only a few words to Robin then shook her head. Robin ran off stage in tears.

"Great," Sara moaned.

"Sara," Erin said. "Never mind Robin! Just go out there and dance." She waited for Sara to agree. "OK?"

"OK," Sara said, thinking of the San Francisco Ballet dancers who would be arriving at the theater soon. As she turned to walk out to the barre, Mr. Moyne appeared in front of her, his face gaudy with stage make-up.

"Are you OK?" Mr. Moyne asked. Sara nodded, though her knees felt weak. "You will dance the part. We told Robin she could dance in the group in her ballet shoes, but I'm not sure if she will," Mr. Moyne told her. "Poor girl," he said.

"Yes," Sara said. "I'm so sorry." Mr. Moyne looked at her quizzically. "For her," Sara quickly added.

"She'll be all right," Mr. Moyne finished. "Better start some warm-ups."

The three of them went to the barre. Soon the orchestra was tuning up, the curtains were closed, and Sara could hear the audience arriving. She could almost feel the hands of the clock moving toward the opening pose, and she heard someone cough on the other side of the curtain. When Miss Sutton said "Places everyone!" Sara felt Erin squeeze her hand and whisper, "Break a leg." Then she was gone to the other side of the stage. Sara quickly took off her sweater and leg warmers and threw them on a chair in the wings. The stagehands removed the barres, and Sara started for her opening position.

Suddenly, she remembered—rosin! She ran back to the wings and quickly pressed the toes and soles of her satin shoes in the shallow box of powder. She ran back to the stage, got into her pose, and the curtains opened. Everything seemed strangely quiet and sharply organized.

As suddenly as the sun had come up that morning, Sara felt the bright stage lights flood over her. Please, let everything be perfect, she thought, taking a deep breath. The audience applauded immediately at the accuracy and beauty of the traditional opening pose. Sara smiled. She could feel a special magic tonight—the electricity of a real performance. The ballet began, and Sara's toes seemed to take her effortlessly across the floor in the tiny bourrée steps she had practiced so long. Her arms moved overhead as softly as her feet moved beneath her, and her fluffy white costume billowed in the breeze of the other dancers. It seemed easy to stay in rhythm with the whole company as they moved into two large circles at either side of the stage. Sara could sense everyone's strength, concentration, and grace as she lowered herself carefully to her knee and breathed gently. She felt the entire ensemble moving as one, their arms rising to an arc then down again to the sides of their costumes.

She rose slowly with the others, moved into a straight line facing off-stage, and posed with one leg behind. As the first soloist leaped onto the stage, Sara moved her arms lightly out and in, watching the dancer out of the corner of her eye. The soloist was higher in the air than she was at rehearsal, and Sara's heart beat with inspiration.

Then it was time for her special part. She counted five, six, seven, eight, and ran out to Mr. Moyne. Suddenly she heard Miss Abbey say, "No matter how small a part, the dancer has a responsibility to make it larger by the way she dances it." She smiled and became the graceful fairy she had imagined in her vision. She felt light and happy doing the waltz steps, then joyous in the air for the lifts. Mr. Moyne seemed charged with energy, and she soared above him higher than she ever had. She breathed in forever, stretched her legs long, and held her head high. As Mr. Moyne carried her off-stage into the wings, the audience broke into applause. *For me*, Sara's heart whispered! *The whole audience is applauding for me!*

She hurried back onstage and took her place in the ensemble, but she felt different. She was aware of being more relaxed and confident, like she was a leader even though she was doing the same movements as everyone else. She noticed every detail around her from the softly moving fingers and little wisps of neck hair on the girl next to her, to the stage lights flowing through the tiny holes in the white net costumes. She felt awake, but part of a dream. It was just as Madame had said it would be—poetic, wonderful, magical.

The ballet ended in the same perfect pose with which it had opened, and the velvet curtains drew closed in front of them to thunderous applause. Sara quickly ran through a jumble of dancers and found her place for bows, holding the hands of the girls on either side. When the curtains opened Sara smiled, ran forward with the others in her line, placed her foot back, and curtsied. The line split, ran off to the sides, and entered again, behind the others. After each line had taken its turn, Sara ran out to meet Mr. Moyne for her special bow, smiling excitedly as he took her hand. She curtsied graciously while the audience applauded and the warm lights shined on her face. Mr. Moyne's smile confirmed that everything had gone well, and Sara felt herself glow with happiness.

After the soloists took their bows, a senior dancer presented Miss Sutton and Madame with bouquets of flowers. Then the curtain closed for the last time. After all the long rehearsals and the worry, after the exciting performance itself, it was simply over. Everyone scattered in all directions. "Sara!" Erin ran over from the other side of the stage. They threw their arms around each other. "You were great!" Erin beamed.

"Finally!" Sara said. She was just so happy. They made their way off-stage and through the hall to the dressing room. Someone had placed performance programs for them at their places, and Sara and Erin found flowers on their chairs.

"From my mom and dad!" Erin exclaimed, holding up red carnations and roses.

Sara read her card: "To my very special daughter and wonderful dancer, with all my love—Mom." She opened the paper to find six beautiful yellow roses in a fairy's dream of baby's breath. A wide yellow ribbon held them together. She felt a lump in her throat wishing her mom had seen the performance.

"Let's hurry and get these in water!" Erin said.

"I can't believe it's over and I can't believe I was in it!" Sara said.

Erin picked up one of the programs. "Well," she smiled, "my feet know I was in it and this program proves it!"

Sara took three of the programs. One for her mom, one for Jen, and one for herself. She would put hers in the red tin along with Jen's letters. She put two of them in her dance bag and held the one that would always be hers. *Lakewood Dance Camp presents "**Les Sylphides**" Saturday, July 30 at 8 pm.* She opened it. There was her name set off by itself for the special part—*my* part, she finally let herself say. She smiled as she cut the stitches from her pink ribbons and let them unfurl.

CHAPTER TWENTY-TWO

"Master Class"

"Yuri Pashchenko!" Sara exclaimed as she stared at the notice posted on the studio door. The dancer she'd seen in the dance magazine would be teaching her master class! On the other side of the door, the piano beat out a steady rhythm for the senior class, and Sara could feel the floor vibrate as she sat down in the hallway to stretch.

"How do you think he pronounces his name?" Erin asked, pulling her knee up to her shoulder.

"Yuri," Sara laughed.

"I mean his *last* name," Erin said.

"I don't know. Yuri is good enough for me." Suddenly, a burst of applause rang out in the studio. The door opened and the dancers walked between the intermediates to the dressing room mopping their brows.

Sara's heart beat fast as she slipped through the door. She was nervous but not really scared like she had been at the audition class. She was here today already chosen for Class A with the *Sylphides* performance under her belt. She was picturing her yellow roses when Erin nudged her. Yuri had entered the room.

His bone structure was delicate, his face open and soft, his legs muscular. I want to know everything he knows, everything you have to know to become a real dancer, Sara thought.

"We begin," Yuri said, nodding to the accompanist. His instructions were crystal clear, his corrections fair, his face encouraging, his choreography joyful. Sara felt she could dance for him forever. After demonstrating a fast combination across the floor with high leaps and turns, Yuri suddenly pointed to Erin, Sara, Lin Tan, and Kathy Jacobs. "First group!" he directed.

Uh-oh, Sara thought. She knew Yuri must see her as one of the top dancers in the class to put her in the first group to go across the floor. But it also meant there was no opportunity to see the combination again. She'd have to get her body muscles to remember it immediately. To play it safe, she took a place in the back line of the little group, and went over the movement sequence in her mind as the piano gave them an introduction. Lin lead the group in the front line, and Sara tried to watch her out of the corner of her eye, but Yuri's choreography seemed to be made just for Sara. Dancing it was a light, nearly miraculous experience that she performed confidently and with expression.

During the pointe work, Yuri took the class through rises on pointe, échappés, turns, and arabesques on relevé. Robin sat out, rubbing her injured foot. It would be a while before she'd be able to dance full out or get back on her pointe shoes. Sara felt terrible about it, but noticed there seemed to be much more space available for her own dancing. She filled it with exuberance.

Yuri expected them to be as soft as wood nymphs and as fluid as sprites beneath the sea. He brought Lin forward to have her demonstrate the combination of strength and softness he expected. When Sara did her bourrées for him, she was sure they had never been more graceful. Her leaps soared at the end of class, the notes of the piano carrying her up and up. She felt content when she bowed her grand réverénce, and though she was tired, she wished the class could go on longer. Yuri smiled as the class applauded for him, then gave a little bow. Sara couldn't wait to see him dance in *Swan Lake*.

As the class headed for the door, Miss Sutton raised her hand. "Just a couple of announcements." Sara watched Yuri make his exit. "I want to congratulate those of you who were in the performance last night." The class applauded and cheered. "Photos from dress rehearsal will be available for you to purchase next week. And for those of you who danced in the performance, we will show the film of it this afternoon in the studio after lunch. That's all dancers," Miss Sutton said, excusing them. "I'll see everyone in the Balanchine Theater at three o'clock for *Swan Lake!*"

At lunch, while Sara floated in the excitement of last night's performance and the wonderful master class, Becky was talking about going horseback riding with the boys. "Mary will let us go if our whole cabin agrees," she said.

Danielle looked at Sara and Erin. "You want to go, right? Because if you don't," she said, "We won't get any rest from this cowgirl!"

Sara was amazed that anyone could get so excited about horses. And she wondered if Robin would agree to go.

"Sure," Erin said. "We want to go."

Sara guessed that Erin was thinking of being with Paul, but it was the right answer anyway because Becky was so enthusiastic.

After lunch, Becky and Danielle took the path to the cabin, and Sara and Erin went back to the studio to watch the performance film. When the curtain opened and the music began,

Sara's mouth dropped. It was beautiful, gorgeous, tremendous, spectacular! She watched in awe as she blended gracefully with the other dancers, identical in their costumes and make-up. The luscious white gowns billowed across the stage, every head turning at exactly the same moment, every arm moving together. Sara held her breath as she watched herself run out to meet the Mr. Moyne. They waltzed as if in a dream, then he lifted her effortlessly above him, her skirt flowing. As he carried her off into the wings Sara heard the audience applaud for her again.

"See?" Erin nudged her. "You were great!" They took off for the cabin to freshen-up before going to *Swan Lake*. But they opened the door to find Robin crying and Hillary handing her Kleenex.

"Robin?" Erin said. "What's wrong?"

Robin sat up, her strawberry curls going every which way. "Did you see that performance?" she cried. "I looked awful! Like some junior beginner without my pointe shoes on trying to pretend everything was fine."

Sara hadn't noticed that at all. "No, Robin," she said. "It looked great. Everyone looked the same."

Robin glared at her. "I looked so bad, I couldn't even stay to watch it. And that banner," she said, pointing to the wall. "Break a leg—just what I wanted to see!"

Sara glanced at the banner. It was even splashier now that Becky and Danielle had written "Congrats" and "Great Job! across it. "My friend sent it to me for good luck," she said.

"Well, I'm not having any," Robin sniffled.

"Mary said yes!" Becky let the screen door slam. "We can go riding! Everyone wants to go, right?"

Robin looked up.

"With the boys?" Hillary asked.

"Yes," Becky said. "And their horses!"

Robin stood up and blew her nose. "Cool," she said. "Hillary and I will go." She went into the bathroom. Sara was amazed.

"It's going to be next Sunday," Becky said. "I can't wait!"

"Sounds good," Robin said from the bathroom. She splashed cold water on her face and came out with her hair brushed back. You couldn't tell she'd been crying. "Let's get going or we'll be late for *Swan Lake*." Sara looked at Erin. Erin shrugged, and they followed Robin out the door.

CHAPTER TWENTY-THREE

"Swan Lake"

Sara sat in the theater reviewing her program. She wanted to read every word about every dancer. The company photos were divided into groups of Principal Dancers, Soloists, Corps De Ballet, and Apprentices. There were only four apprentices listed and Sara wondered how old they were, how they got chosen, and how they might be promoted into the Corps. She found Yuri's picture in the section for Principal Dancers, and his name listed as Prince Siegfried for today's performance. Yuan Wu, originally from China, was going to dance the part of Odette, the beautiful Swan Queen. All the women they had seen through the studio windows rehearsing yesterday would be the wonderful ensemble of Swan Maidens.

"The dancers are from all over the world," Erin exclaimed. "China, Spain, Russia, even Norway!"

"I know," Sara said. She realized how competitive it would be to get into a world-class company. The program notes explained the Second Act that they would see today: *The prince is hunting with his crossbow near a lake when one of the swans turns into a beautiful woman, Odette. He is immediately captivated by her, but she*

111

is frightened of him and tells him she and the other swans are under a wicked magician's spell. By day they are swans—it is only at night they can become human again. The spell can only be broken if a man promises his love and remains faithful to his vow. The young prince falls in love with the woman but the wicked magician appears. When the prince tries to kill him Odette interferes, knowing that if the magician dies before the spell is broken she will have to remain a swan forever. The wicked magician escapes, and Odette runs away.

Sara noted that the Second Act contained the beautiful waltz, the quick dance of the four little cygnets, and the remarkable pas de deux, the dance for two, by Odette and Prince Siegfried all danced to the stirring music of Tchaikovsky. As dawn broke at the lakeside scene the maidens would have to become swans again, and Odette would bid the prince a tender farewell turning again into the Swan Queen. But the prince would vow to love her forever, and no other woman, and this would break the spell. It was SO romantic.

Sara was riveted in silence for the entire performance. Rows and rows of dancers up on their toes, quivering in place, their arms, backs, and necks convincing the audience they were swans. Yuri made a strong, handsome, but sensitive prince, not wanting to scare the beautiful Swan Queen. He partnered her with strength and grace. And Yuan Wu was perfection itself, a real queen who seemed a real swan too. Sara had never seen such an inspiring combination of strong dancing and soft expression. She had a lump in her throat at the end as she stood on her feet clapping. She yearned to be part of such a great company and promised herself she would be one day.

When the curtain finally closed Sara fell back into her chair and looked at Erin in awe. They let the others push past them on their way out.

"That was amazing!" Sara said when she could speak.

"I know," Erin agreed. "Can you believe we took class from Yuri this morning?"

"I can't," she said, knowing she'd never be able to find words to describe her feelings. She wanted to be a swan dancing bourrées in place, her back arched, her head tilted up toward the sky, mist around her feet. She got up and began to push her arms in and out like the swans. Erin joined her and they left the theater dancing up the aisle. When they got into the sunlight, they took off running, clutching their programs to their chests.

That night in bed Sara held her program next to the window and managed to read in a bit of moonlight: *The Act 2 Swan Lake danced by most companies everywhere is from the St. Petersburg, Russia version staged January 27, 1895. Russian George Balanchine staged it in his own choreography for his New York City Ballet in 1951.*

Sara got chills thinking how she had just been in the theater named for Balanchine, sitting next to Erin who took her classes at the school of the New York City Ballet, watching a Russian ballet Balanchine had once staged.

She closed her program and lay back on the bed, moonlight playing on her cheek. She felt the heritage of great ballet weaving through her, connecting her to the ancient spirits of dance. She was like a single shiny pearl strung onto the beautiful necklace of all of classical ballet. Her pearl contained Madame's classes, her performance in *Les Sylphides,* the master class with Yuri, and *Swan Lake.* She looked back to her first day at camp, meeting Erin, the opening ceremony, class auditions. It seemed so far away. She was exactly in the center of the most important summer of her life. It was like standing in the middle of a river she had to finish crossing. A dapple of moonlight caressed her hand as she felt for the pearls on her neck. But only her locket was there.

CHAPTER TWENTY-FOUR

"Sara's Great Plan"

Monday morning Sara woke up with a plan. In the evenings she and Erin would practice modern and tap. There were only four weeks until the end of camp and the announcement of the scholarship winners. She promised herself today would be the day she started concentrating even harder in Miss Casey's modern class, now that *Les Sylphides* was over and the San Francisco Ballet had gone. She looked at her yellow roses on the dresser. When they died she would press them in a book, then put them in the red tin along with her letters from Jen and the programs from *Les Sylphides* and *Swan Lake.*

"Aren't I getting better in tap?" Erin asked at lunch.

"Definitely," Sara said. "But you have to get even better. I thought we agreed on all this."

"I know," Erin said. "But it's good to have some down time after all the rehearsals for *Sylphides.*"

"I don't think there is down time for scholarship winners," Sara said. "Besides, I still need your help with modern."

"OK," Erin said. "But I don't want to start until tomorrow."

"OK," Sara agreed.

But at the end of modern class, Miss Casey announced the Lakewood Student Dance Concert. It was for the Intermediate Division only. They could do any kind of dance they wanted, and it could be a solo or a group number, but they had to create their own choreography or perform an authentic solo dance from a classic ballet.

"The performance will be Saturday evening, August 13," Miss Casey said. "The dance building will be open evenings until nine for you to rehearse. Sign up with me to visit the costume room. You can go to the music library any time to check out music."

Evening rehearsals. Sara looked down at her bare feet. There goes my great plan, she thought. With only two weeks until the student concert and four weeks until the end of camp, how would they find time for their private practices? She'd have to talk Erin into weekends now.

Miss Casey added, "The boys from Will-O-Green are invited to the concert and an ice cream party afterward. It's going to be really fun."

Really fun? Sara thought. My great plan destroyed and Hank watching me dance something I have to make up and don't have a clue about yet is supposed to be really fun?

Sara and Erin stood in the costume room the next morning gazing at rows of old costumes, the smell of dust and fabrics filling the air. Sara's eyes held the wonder of sequins, ribbons, feathers, bows, velvet, satin, and netting.

"Here's a Sugar Plum Fairy costume!" Erin hollered over the top of a clothes rack. "It's gorgeous."

"That is beautiful!" Sara said. "But do you know the Sugar Plum Fairy variation?"

"No," Erin admitted. "But we could make something up different to go with the costume. Please? I really want to wear this costume."

"When I dance Sugar Plum Fairy it's going to be the real choreography from *Nutcracker*. Besides, there's only one costume and we shouldn't do ballet. Everyone will do ballet."

"Here's something," Erin called from down the aisle. She was holding up a red satin jacket. Sara could imagine the luster it would have under stage lights.

"Is there another one?" Sara asked, going over to feel the soft material.

"Yeah," Erin said. "There's a bunch. Must have been a big tap number."

"YES!" Sara said. "Tap! We can wear these jackets over black leotards with baggy pants and have little hats. Maybe we could find some Broadway jazz music. Tap!" She was already making up the steps in her mind.

But Erin looked dismayed. "I thought we could wear the jackets over red leotards and do pointe," she said. "Tap is my worst thing."

"I know, but you're improving every day. And it would be really different! Hardly anyone else will do tap! Come on," she said. "Let's find some pants." She went into the main aisle, glancing down the rows.

"Hey, what about these?" Erin yelled from two rows back. She held up sand colored leotards and tights that had been brushed with thick strokes of green, yellow, and maroon paint. There were long scarves to match.

"Those are gorgeous, but not for tap," Sara said. She had to admit they were beautiful.

"I know," Erin said. "But I really want to do ballet."

117

Oh, she's probably right, Sara thought. She's not that good in tap yet. I'd really have to help her a lot. Help her a lot... That gave her an idea. She went to the painted costumes and started going through them all to find the two best ones. "I know!" she said. "Let's wear these and do modern dance."

"YES!" Erin smiled. "But I'll really have to help you a lot."

Exactly, Sara thought. It was what her mother called killing two birds with one stone.

PART TWO

CHAPTER TWENTY-FIVE

"Snowflakes in Summer"

Three beautiful velvet costumes trimmed in white fur were hanging on the wall in the ballet studio Wednesday morning. Furry white muffs hung from each one, and white hats to match rested on the piano.

"We do *Les Patineurs* for final concert. Is French to mean the skaters," Madame told them. "You pretend to ice skate," she said. "I choreograph for you and Class B together. Is ballet from long time ago. Half to wear red, other half blue, a few to wear white," Madame continued. "Lots of parts for everybody. We begin to learn in class. Also, we rehearse in big studio with Class B on weekend."

Sara was sure Madame meant "weekends"—the only real time left for their private tap and modern practices. And she would definitely need the extra help with modern now for the student concert performance. She just had to get a scholarship.

Before they began their pliés, Madame added, "Special surprise! Paper snowflakes to fall on stage. Snowflakes in summer! Fifty girls in snow on big outdoor stage on lake." She was absolutely cheery.

Sara loved the quick and lively music for the ballet. She was paired with Erin for the sliding entrance step, their arms crossed like real skating partners. When the class had practiced it to perfection, Madame taught them a combination of tricky footwork that twisted back on itself in quick changes of direction.

After they repeated the choreography several times, Madame asked them to dance it on their pointe shoes. Robin sat out. Madame watched intently as the class struggled through the challenging combination. Then she called Sara, Erin, and Robin, along with Lin and Kathy to dance it alone. Robin looked surprised and joined them center-floor as the rest of the class stepped back along the barres.

"You do combination," she instructed. "Make two lines." Sara put herself in the back line, afraid of making mistakes that might confuse the other dancers. But when the music took them through the movements, no one did it perfectly as far as she could see. Sara looked at the group in the mirror as they danced it again. Tiny-boned Lin was crisp. Erin was soft, flowing, and light. Robin was aggressive and a little ahead of the music. Kathy held her own.

Then Madame asked Robin, Lin, and Kathy to do it as a trio. Sara watched carefully, trying to understand it better. She thought she had it when Madame called on her to repeat it, this time with Erin and Lin. But at the end of it, she and Lin were standing on different feet with different arms up, and Sara didn't know who was right. She watched again as Robin repeated it with Kathy.

Madame called Sara back with Robin, Lin, and Kathy. Sara was sure they were auditioning for the special parts for the four white costumes. She felt the pressure of getting the steps perfect this time. But, again, not everyone ended up with the same foot and arm. "If you make a mistake, act like you are the only one doing it right," she could hear Miss Abbey saying. Madame asked her to stay out on the floor with Robin and Lin, then she called Erin to join them. The music began its quick frolic and this time Sara smiled, pretended she was doing everything perfectly, and tried to stay in time with the other dancers. By the time they were at the halfway point, Sara knew they were working well together. At the end they all held identical poses, and the class burst into applause. But Madame kept looking them over. Her eyes roamed over to Kathy at the side of the room, then back to the four in front of her.

"These your four white costumes!" Madame announced. "Pas de quatre! Dance for four!"

Sara and Erin grinned at each other while the class applauded again. Sara looked over to the white costumes and imagined the paper snow falling on them. She could almost feel the stiff net petticoat brushing against her knees. This time it would be her special part from the beginning.

As they left the studio, Madame handed them rehearsal schedules for *Les Patineurs*. Sara glanced at hers as she waited for Erin to finish at the drinking fountain.

"So Robin makes it without auditioning in pointe shoes?" Erin whispered when it was Sara's turn to swallow the cold water.

Erin was right. It didn't really seem fair. But in her heart, Sara felt that Robin really was the strongest, most experienced dancer in their class. She had a self-confidence most of the others didn't have yet.

At lunch, Sara and Erin studied Madame's rehearsal schedule. Sara took a pen and paper out of her dance bag and blocked out a schedule that included their private practices, rehearsals for the student concert, and for *Les Patineurs*. "OK," she said. "Mondays through Thursdays after lunch we help each other with modern and tap until two o'clock. Evenings, we work on our student concert choreography in the dance building from six-thirty to seven-thirty. From seven forty-five until eight forty-five we rehearse with Madame for the pas de quatre. See? It will work!"

"Yeah," Erin moaned. "If we don't collapse. And don't forget, we have rehearsals with Class B on Saturday mornings for *Patineurs*."

Sara wrote that on the sheet, then took a sip of her ice water. She looked up at the clock. "Well, let's go—it's time for our first tap and modern practice!" she said.

CHAPTER TWENTY-SIX

"The Axe Man"

As they walked back to the cabin Sara felt delightfully organized. The cabin was empty, with Becky and Danielle in class and Robin and Hillary outside somewhere. They went right to work. They did modern first, and Sara got to ask lots of questions. It was amazing how quickly she was catching on with a private teacher. She felt she might even grow to love dancing that way. But halfway through their rehearsal, Mary opened the cabin door.

"Hey, you two," she said "Would you take these flyers over to the boys camp headquarters?"

"Sure," Sara answered, taking the stack of bright blue papers for the student dance concert and ice cream party. When Mary left, Erin dove under the bed for the red cookie tin. She opened it, took a cookie out, broke it in half for them, then pulled the foil up and put two of the flyers under it. They threw the tin back under Erin's bunk in the middle of her shoe boxes and took off for the boys camp.

"Let's take the secret path," Erin said. "We're on official business."

They ran to the stand of tall pine trees, then plunged head-long down the skinny path through the thick brush. Sara giggled as she ran faster, letting the steepness going downhill carry her swiftly toward the moist, minty earth and the stream. She heard Erin's feet pounding close behind, then felt the black muck and the cold of the water. When she got to the stream she stopped short, remembering Robin falling through the plank. Erin rushed past her.

"Look!" Erin yelled. "A new board!"

This one was wider and thick enough to hold at least two people. "I wonder who did this," Sara said, walking onto it, clutching the flyers. Erin followed her across. Someone knew what had happened there. David knew, of course, and had told Hank and Paul some of it. She wondered how many other people knew. Suddenly a deep voice burst from the woods.

"Hey!" a man yelled at them, swinging an axe. Sara nearly fell off the board into the water. She didn't know if she should run to the end or turn back. She felt Erin stop behind her. She clung tightly to her flyers, frozen. The man loomed large in front of her now, his face as gruff as his voice. He motioned with his axe for them to continue across. Sara looked back at Erin to see her face flush from fear, then she jumped off the board into the water and took off as fast as she could into the woods. She could hear Erin panting behind her when she finally slowed.

"Where are we?" Erin asked.

"I have no idea," Sara said, trying to get her breath. She looked around for a path.

"That guy was really scary," Erin said.

"Yeah, I noticed," Sara said, wondering how close they came to being newspaper headlines.

They wouldn't be able to tell anyone about him because they weren't supposed to be on this end of the lake, and now they'd have to hurry to find their way to the boys camp a different way. Sara looked up and found a slight clearing in the trees. "This way," she said, pushing her way through low hanging branches.

They found a footpath and took it, listening for voices.

"Look!" Erin said, pointing. Just ahead was the horse barn. They ran full out until they reached it. Sara was trying to catch her breath and organize her flyers when another voice startled her. She jumped back, then realized it was Paul.

"Hi!" Erin smiled. "We're on business." She waved a flyer. "Did you just get back?"

"Yeah, we're trying to get the horses settled," Paul said, taking a flyer. Hank appeared next looking like a cowboy with his lanky legs in old jeans, a red bandana around his neck.

"Hey!" Sara said. "How was the trip?"

"We survived," he said, reading a flyer. "This should be fun."

Yeah fun, Sara thought, worrying about what dance they would do. "We have to give these flyers to somebody at headquarters then get back for class," she said.

"OK," Hank said. "We'll take you there." Then he looked beyond Sara. "Charlie!" he shouted. "We're back with the horses!"

Sara turned to see the man with the axe. Her heart jumped. She looked at Erin. "Oh," she said to Hank, "that's Charlie who sleeps in the horse barn?"

"The one and only!" he answered.

Charlie made his way up the slope toward them, firewood in his arm. "Keep yer shirts on!" he yelled. "The horses know I'm comin'!" He disappeared around the front of the barn.

"Let's go," Hank said. They passed the boats bobbing in the water, walked beyond the fire pit and then behind the dining hall to headquarters. "Here you are!" Hank said. "The brain center of Camp Will-O-Green! I have to get going," he added. "But don't forget about the sailboat races Saturday morning."

"Can't do that one," Sara said. "We have rehearsals Saturday mornings."

"But we're going horseback riding with you guys Sunday," Erin said.

"I don't care if I ever get back on a horse," Paul laughed.

"No, that's really cool," Hank said. "We'll see you then."

"Bye." Sara smiled and let the headquarters door shut between them, then turned and put the flyers on the counter.

They took the long way back. On the way Sara formulated a new worry: What if Charlie had recognized her as the one in the horse barn with Hank the night of the party?

CHAPTER TWENTY-SEVEN

"The Magic of the Mysterious Cabin"

In the morning on the way to pointe class, Sara told Erin of her worry. "But it was so dark in there," she said, "I don't know how he could have gotten a good look at me."

"He probably didn't," Erin said. But Sara knew it was Charlie who got Robin demoted last year by telling someone that he had seen her and David in the barn.

"Do you think it was Charlie who was roaming around our cabin the night Hillary was screaming about it and you went out to look for me?" Erin asked.

That was a scary thought to Sara. She looked at Erin. "I'll tell you one thing, if I see anything again, I'm telling Mary. We don't need Axe Man wandering around over here!"

Erin laughed. "He's not an axe man," she said. "He's just Charlie, and he was out cutting firewood."

"I know," Sara said, "but he shouldn't be cutting it on our side of the lake."

In class, Madame demonstrated a movement that required sudden changes in weight, a falling off balance, and out of control spinning. Everyone laughed. She turned to them. "Is good you laugh," she said. "Is supposed to be funny!" After the class had tried it together to the music, Madame asked Hillary to try it alone. It was remarkable! Hillary threw herself into the role of comic skater without hesitating. When she finished, the class applauded and she bowed to them in a silly way, pretending to slip on ice. Madame let two other girls try the part, but in the end she awarded it to Hillary.

After lunch, Sara took a red colored pen and wrote *Les Patineurs* in big letters on the banner. "We should write something about Hillary's part," she said.

"I will!" Erin said, taking the pen. She wrote "Hillary the Hilarious" and drew a stick figure of a skater about to fall. "There," she said.

Then Sara drew four figures, wrote "Pas de quatre," and labeled the figures Erin, Lin, Robin, and Sara. "We'll put Danielle and Becky's names up here when they get their parts," she said, putting the pen back.

Erin clicked on the music they borrowed from the library, and was taking Sara through the basic modern warm-up exercises when Robin and Hillary came in. First they bumped into them to get to the bathroom, and then Hillary slapped the figure of herself on the banner. "Cool!" she said. Then they got on their bunks to write letters and asked Sara and Erin to keep quiet. "We can't," Sara said. "We're trying to practice."

Robin frowned and kept writing. Hillary was so happy from getting her part in *Les Sylphides* that she began to hum. Sara stared at her.

"Why don't you two go outside and practice?" Robin said. Erin turned off the music.

"Because." Sara said. "We might ..."

"Might what?" Robin said.

130

"Nothing," Sara said. She was going to say they might sprain a foot or something. "Come on, Erin." They went out on the porch.

"You could help me with tap out here," Erin said.

"Tomorrow's tap day," Sara said, feeling overwhelmed. "And I really need your help with modern, too."

"Hang on," Erin said. "We have a place to practice," she whispered. "The old cabin." They took the secret path as far as they needed to, then veered off to the left crossing the stream where it became a rivulet. They found it more easily this time.

The cabin was hot and musty inside from being closed up, yet had a feel like someone else had been there. They swept the acorns aside with an old newspaper and began to practice. The vibrant drum and violin music they had chosen for their modern dance piece filled the old cabin, and Sara seemed to flow easily in the movements. Even the little deer stood at a distance staring at the cabin. Something strange and magical seemed to be helping Sara dance in these woods. She thought she felt the pearls around her neck again over her locket. They were careful to close all the windows and doors when they left.

That night at student concert rehearsal Sara tried to focus on the new movement Erin was showing her, but she was distracted by the other dancers in the big studio. Across the room, Becky and Danielle were working on a very cool jazz number. Near them Kathy Jacobs was making up a sharp tap routine, and others were working out ballet dances to lyrical music.

"Come on, Sara," Erin said. "We need to get more of this done if we're going to get it finished on schedule." They had agreed the piece should be finished by Monday when their evening rehearsals for the *Les Patineurs* pas de quatre would begin. That would give them enough time to polish it for the concert.

131

"I just wish there were real steps for modern dance like in tap or ballet," Sara said. In spite of their good afternoon practice, she was frustrated now trying to learn a flow of motion to Erin's counting.

"Well, steps or no steps, we only have three days to finish it," Erin said.

They decided to take a break downstairs where it was cool. On the way to the locker room, they glanced into the small studio to see Robin and Hillary rehearsing at the far end of the room. Lin sat on the floor watching. "Wow," Sara said. It was a modern dance piece to lilting flute music. Robin and Hillary's bodies were moving gracefully, leaning into each other, and rolling and leaping freely. Sara couldn't believe how much they had finished already and how well they did it. "We have to look that good," Sara whispered to Erin, "if we want points toward a scholarship."

"I don't think they're giving any points toward the scholarships for the student concert," Erin said. "It's just for fun."

"Well, maybe not real points, but they'll keep it in their minds," Sara said, sure it was true. "Our dance has to be more exciting." Trouble was, she wasn't sure how to make it that way.

CHAPTER TWENTY-EIGHT

"Everything Counts"

Saturday morning all fifty intermediates gathered in the big studio for *Les Patineurs*. Sara looked through the windows to the lake where she could see the boys' sailboats lining up in the wind for the race. Go Will-0-Way, she secretly cheered. Danielle won a short solo and skated her way across the studio to her classmates' cheers. Madame had a gift for making movements perfectly suited to each dancer, and Sara couldn't wait until Monday to see what Madame had in mind for the pas de quatre.

They practiced most of the morning on the entrance step, with Erin and Sara leading half the paired dancers in from one side, and Robin and Lin leading the other half in from across the stage. They pretended to skate toward each other, then formed one big circle. It was like skating around a pond in winter, but called for the utmost in teamwork because they had to hang onto the girl's waist in front of them.

"Spacing!" Madame repeated each time the circle broke apart. "Keep arms outstretched. Not pull girl in front." Robin was behind Sara, Erin was in front of her, and she felt like an accordion squeezed between them. Her arms kept getting pulled out too hard or getting completely scrunched. Madame excused them saying she was sure they would get it right soon. She always said that even while she kept pouring on new choreography. Sara noted that Kathy Jacobs had been given a beautiful long solo, though she hadn't made it into the pas de quatre.

"Let's put Danielle on the banner for her solo in *Les Patineurs*!" Becky said after lunch. Though Danielle insisted it wasn't a real solo, just a small part, Becky found the red marker on the chest of drawers and wrote "Danielle—Solo" on the paper near the other names and drew a figure like an ice skater. "There!" she said. "Hurray for Danielle!"

Sara clapped with the others and hugged Danielle. "Good goin'!" she said. "You're going to be great!" Then she realized that Becky was the only one not on the banner yet. "You'll be next!" she told her.

"Yeah," Erin said. "You'll probably get your part Monday."

"Yeah," Becky said. "But my real fun's going to be horse-back riding tomorrow. Yahoo!"

That night Sara and Erin went to the dance building to work on their student concert piece. Dress rehearsal was five days away, and they had to come up with something truly imaginative. But everything they tried seemed awkward or boring.

"I don't like that," Erin kept saying to Sara's ideas, though she didn't have any great ones of her own. After an hour they had added several movements, but Sara was not excited about them. "The important thing is we're moving toward completion," Erin said as they went downstairs for a break. "And I love our music."

But Sara wanted more than just completion. She couldn't shake the vision of how good Robin and Hillary's dance was.

134

She looked in the small studio to catch some of their rehearsal, but tonight they were sitting on the floor watching Lin. Sara and Erin watched from the doorway as Lin, in pointe shoes and a short white practice tutu, performed intricate movements. The music is so beautiful and familiar, Sara thought, immediately captivated by Lin's dancing.

"Oh my gosh!" Erin whispered. "She's doing Sugar Plum Fairy!"

That's it! Sara thought. It's the music from *Nutcracker.* She watched Lin's movements more closely. It looked like she was doing the authentic steps.

"She's going to wear that gorgeous costume!" Erin said. "The one I wanted to wear."

"Shhh," Robin said, turning her eyes to them, then back to Lin.

"I'm going to get a drink," Erin whispered.

Sara's eyes were glued to the rehearsal. When Lin finished what she knew, Robin and Hillary applauded and Lin walked across the room to stop a practice film. She was learning the movements from a film of *Nutcracker*! It was going to be so good! It was going to be authentic, the real thing, in the real costume, with the real music. Sara was still standing in the doorway when Erin came back. She pointed to the monitor indicating the film that Lin had stopped. Then Lin came toward them, wiping her forehead with a little towel.

"It looks really good," Sara told her.

"Thank you," Lin said, pushing back a strand of black hair. "I am working hard." She went to the fountain, her little feet turned out like a duck, the tutu skirt bouncing. Sara was seriously worried now. How would they get their modern piece to the point of competing with that?

"I told you, Sara," Erin insisted in the locker room. "The Student Dance Concert is not a competition."

"Look, Erin," Sara suddenly exploded. "Your father is your father, not a divorced ghost. And he's a doctor who can afford to send you back here next summer and the summer after that. The only way I'm coming back here next summer is by winning a scholarship— everything I do counts!"

"Well, you can count by yourself for the rest of the night!" Erin shouted back. "I'm out of here." She walked away. Sara stood there alone in crying in anger. Finally, she slammed her locker door and left.

CHAPTER TWENTY- NINE

"The Horseback Ride"

Becky had set the alarm for six and was having a blast waking everybody up. "Calling all cowgirls! Calling all cowgirls!" she yelled from the top of her bunk, pulling the chain to the light bulb off and on. Sara stared at her and moaned. "The bus is leavin' soon for the Will-O-Green Ranch," Becky said. "So if you want to eat you better get crackin'."

"What time is it?" Danielle's voice came out from under her covers.

"Time to get goin'!" Becky smiled, giving the chain another pull.

Sara hadn't seen Becky like this before. It was how Sara felt about dance. She thought only a moment about last night's rehearsal before she climbed out of bed. Erin was deep in sleep and probably not ready to forgive her. She'd go to breakfast with Becky. Everyone straggled in and Mary told them over her coffee that Mr. Field and the boys would meet them under the "Will-O-Green" sign and take them to the horse barn. "Have fun, and be back in time for lunch," she said.

"I just hope these cowgirls wake up before they have to sit in a saddle!" Becky laughed.

In the barn Hank helped Sara onto a pretty white horse. "His name's Jake," he said, handing Sara the reins. "And he's spirited like you," he smiled. He tightened her stirrups, then got on Rosie, his black horse. "Let's go," Hank said, riding past her. Jake needed only a nudge to get going and seemed to follow Rosie into the sunlight as a matter of course. Sara wasn't an experienced rider and hoped the horses would just follow the trail through the woods. Outside, the other horses gathered with their riders mounted and ready to go. Mr. Field rode out of the barn on a tall blond steed with Becky and Danielle on chestnut mares right behind him.

"OK everybody," Mr. Field said. "Stay on the trails. The main one meanders in a big circle through several miles of woods. The boys are familiar with the side trails, but try not to go too far off the main path. Let's head out!" he said, taking the lead. The trail was only wide enough for one horse, so the pack moved slowly single-file with Hank and Sara last. After a while Sara relaxed and gazed into the thickening woods. The sun filtered through lacy tree branches and birds fluttered. The riders grew farther apart on the trail.

"Hey," Hank said. "Here's a nice side path we could take." Soon they were alone. Hank got off Rosie, looped the reins around a tree branch, and helped Sara dismount. Then he took her hand and found a tree stump for them to sit on.

"So who won the sailboat race yesterday?" Sara asked.

"Salty and Skipper beat the Red Clipper!" Hank grinned.

"The Red Clipper is David's boat?" Sara asked.

"Yep. And he's not taking it too well that we took the trophy from him. He was champ three years running."

"Good for you!" Sara said. "I think it's important to win."

"I think it's important to try your best and have fun," Hank said.

"Yeah, but sometimes your life can change if you win," Sara said

"Sometimes your life can change if you don't win," Hank smiled.

But maybe not in the way you'd like, Sara thought.

"Do you like poetry?" Hank asked.

"Well, right now I don't have time for anything like that," Sara said. "I'm totally into dance."

Hank looked a bit disappointed. "Oh," he said. "I thought maybe you..." Without finishing he got up. "Come on," he said as though he had a surprise.

They rode farther into the woods on the side trail until they came to a creek where the horses could drink. It seemed familiar to Sara. Then she saw the mysterious old cabin. "Where are we?" she asked, trying to get her bearings.

"Not that far from Lakewood," Hank said pointing. "It's right over there." Sara looked but saw nothing but thick trees and underbrush.

"So, is this cabin on your side or the girls' side?" Sara asked.

"It's sort of borderline, I guess," Hank said.

"Who would come here?" Erin asked.

"Probably no one in summer," Hank said. "Maybe a deer hunter in winter. Isn't it cool?"

"Yeah," Sara said. "I wonder how long it's been here."

"I don't know," Hank said. "But it could be on sacred ground. Four or five Native American Indian tribes lived around here at one time."

Sacred ground, Sara thought, breathing in deeply. She thought of the mystical sensation in the cabin and the little deer that seemed to lead her when she was lost in the woods.

"We better get back to the main trail," Hank said. They took a short cut back and joined the group. The main trail led them deep into the woods. The longer they were on it, the more Sara wondered if it would ever lead them back home. Then Becky gave a hoot and raced into a clearing. When the others whooped and followed, Sara felt Jake trying to dart out from under her. She tightened the reins, but he didn't want to obey. She could feel Rosie trying to pass, and Jake pulling against the reins, but she was terrified that Jake wouldn't stop if she let him tear away beneath her. "OK, boy," she finally said, holding her breath. "Let's go." The horse careened ahead, and before Sara knew what had happened they were across the clearing and at the end of the trail. Her heart raced as fast as Jake had run.

Safe in the barn, Sara dismounted. "The horses were just making a b-line back to the barn," Becky told her.

"A clue would have been nice," Sara said, still a bit shaken. She felt an arm around her and heard David's voice.

"At least I didn't have to rescue you," David laughed.

"At least," Sara said uneasily as she moved away from him. But Robin was staring at her from the doorway.

CHAPTER THIRTY

"Romeo and Juliet"

"One, two, three, four, and five, six, seven, eight," Erin called out that evening watching Sara dance. She was back to counting and they were talking again, but the modern piece still wasn't spectacular, and rehearsals for the pas de quatre would begin the next night, shortening their time to work on it.

"We are SO stuck!" Sara said.

"We'll get it done," Erin said. "Let's do it again."

But Sara thought big magic was going to have to happen for them to be ready for dress rehearsal Friday night. The boys would be in the audience Saturday, and anyway, it just had to be the best. She thought of Lin's Sugar Plum Fairy variation and Robin and Hillary's modern dance piece, and what she had seen of Kathy's tap number.

When they had exhausted themselves repeating the movements to counting, they turned on the music. It wasn't bad, but they were still only three quarters of the way through the dance. When they came up for air they realized it was after nine and everyone else had gone. "We are SO stuck!" Sara said again in the locker room.

"Shhhh," Erin said. "Listen."

Sara heard faint music drifting down the hall. They went in their practice clothes and bare feet toward the music. It led them past the costume room to a door they didn't remember. They opened it and stood in a dark hallway that led to another door. Light and music seeped from beneath it. Sara was taller, so she peeked into the tiny window in the door. Mr. Moyne and Miss Casey were rehearsing! "Wow," she whispered.

"Let me see," Erin said. Sara gave her a boost. "*Romeo and Juliet*!" Erin whispered.

Yes, that was the music! Sara looked again. She was amazed to see Miss Casey on pointe in a long practice tutu, Mr. Moyne supporting her in pirouettes. To be a real dancer, Sara understood, you had to do all forms of dance. She thought of Miss Casey's feet being like her own, half ballet and half modern. "Art thou tired, sweet Juliet?" Mr. Moyne said. "The hour is late." Miss Casey curtsied to him and clicked off the music. They headed toward the door. Sara grabbed Erin and ran down the hall for the exit door, but the knob slipped. The lights went out behind them and they heard the door click shut. Sara tried the knob again and this time it turned. They ran down the long hall to the locker room, shut the door, and held their breath. When they heard Mr. Moyne and Miss Casey go up the stairs and out the door, they burst out laughing. It was definitely a red tin secret.

"Art thou tired, sweet Juliet?" Erin giggled on the way to the cabin.

"The hour is late," Sara laughed. They bowed to each other, and ran down the path to the cabin. But they were unprepared for what they saw when they got there.

CHAPTER THIRTY-ONE

"Choose Again"

"What are you doing in our costumes?" Sara gasped. "These aren't yours!" Robin said. But she and Hillary were definitely dressed in the brightly painted leotards.

"Yes, they are," Erin said. "Those are our costumes for the student concert."

"No. They're *our* costumes for the student concert," Robin said.

"Like Robin's costume is going to fit either of you?" Hillary said.

Sara and Erin stared at each other. Sara went to her drawer and opened it to find her painted costume. Erin pulled hers out of her dance bag. Now Robin and Hillary were staring.

"Well, you'll have to choose again." Robin said.

"Why us?" Sara said.

"Because our dance is practically finished. We only need a couple more movements," Robin said. "From what I've seen, you two have a long way to go. You could switch costumes."

"Yeah," Hillary said. "Maybe it would inspire you."

Sara couldn't believe it. Inspire them? How about it would smash everything to smithereens? It would ruin her life forever? It would make it impossible to have ANYTHING ready for the concert? They simply had to own them, and wearing them was owning them. "As long as everyone's trying on costumes," she said to Erin, "we will, too!" They marched into the bathroom and came out in the costumes, the long painted scarves tied around their waists.

"Great," Hillary laughed. "You don't even know how to wear them!"

"Look," Robin said. She and Hillary tied their scarves around their heads like exotic turbans, tucking them under at the back.

"Wow!" Erin said. "That looks so cool!" She wrapped hers and tucked it in.

Sara felt silly with her scarf dangling near her feet. She wondered how she was going to keep from tripping, anyway. She put it around her head and looked in the mirror. OK. But now even if they won the battle to wear the costumes, they wouldn't be able to wear the scarves that way since it was Robin's idea. We are REALLY stuck, she thought. She turned away from the mirror and took in the whole picture. The four of them looked *very* cool together. All that beautiful painted color swirling on the stage at once was the spectacular effect she was hoping for. Sara took a breath. "I have an idea," she said. "Let's dance together!"

"Oh, sure," Robin said. "Then you won't have to do the work, just learn ours."

"No," Sara said, taking a chance. "We don't like all of yours. And we definitely like our music better."

"We really love your music," Hillary said.

"Wait a minute," Robin said. "What part of our dance don't you like?"

Sara tried to remember their choreography. "Do you have your music here?" she asked. "Show us your dance, and we'll tell you the parts." Hillary plugged in her player and started the gentle flute music. They began dancing as best they could in the small space. Sara chose a part at random. "Right there," she said. "Try this instead." She offered part of Erin's choreography.

"That looks great!" Erin said.

Sara repeated exchanging movements in a few more places, and then clicked off the flute music. "Now try it to our music," she said, turning on their music. The pulsing sound of drums and violins filled the cabin and Robin couldn't resist. No one could have. The African contemporary music was the blood pumping through your veins, your own heart beating. They mixed it up and strung together movements from the two dances to fit the music. Danielle and Becky came in and stared in appreciation. When the dancers finished, Becky hooted like she was riding a horse.

"That is awesome!" Danielle said. "How long have you guys been working on this?"

"We haven't been," Robin said. "But I think we're going to start tomorrow."

Yes! Sara thought. There was hope.

CHAPTER THIRTY-TWO

"Crack-the-Whip"

"Look, here's you!" Erin yelled to Sara looking up at photos from *Les Sylphides*. The black and white glossies were hanging on the dance building walls when they arrived Monday morning. Sara made her way down the hall through a group of seniors. When she looked at the photo, she was pleased. She was high above Mr. Moyne's head, her beautiful white costume flowing between her legs.

"You have to get it!" Erin said. Sara wrote down the number and also the number for a photo of the opening pose. Then her eye caught some photos from their master class with Yuri. She barely remembered the photographer being in the room, but there was Yuri watching her small group dance across the floor. As she jotted the number, she felt the joy again. They purchased the photos at the dance office and put them in their lockers before going to Madame's class.

"We do entrance step and first section of *Les Patineurs* all together," Madame directed. Sara felt like an accordion again during the big circle. Even with just the twenty-five girls in her class, her arms kept getting scrunched or stretched so she had to

147

let go of Erin's waist. And behind her, Robin kept whispering for her to stay closer. The tempo of the music was so fast and the footwork so tricky that Sara wondered how they would ever do it right with all fifty dancers. When the circle step ended this time Madame made sure that Sara, Erin, Robin, and Lin were in the middle of the line facing the audience. It was where the pas de quatre would begin, and they would start learning it that night. But as they filed out of the room, Madame said, "No pas de quatre rehearsal tonight. Will be only Tuesday and Thursday this week because of other concert you do."

"Perfect!" Sara said to Erin as they hurried to tap class. "We can have long rehearsals with Robin and Hillary tonight and Wednesday night!"

"And shorter ones Tuesday and Thursday," Erin said. They would get unstuck.

"I got my part in *Patineurs!*" Becky said after dinner. She showed it to them in the cabin. "Well, it's not exactly *my* part," she said. "I'm with seven other girls. It's called crack-the-whip. We snap around trying to hold on to each other, and some of us fall down."

"Great. I'll put you on the banner," Hillary said. She drew eight dancers, but Becky was the largest and had radiant lines around her. She wrote "Becky!" underneath. "You're the star of the part," she announced.

"Let's see your photos from *Sylphides*," Robin said to Sara and Erin. Sara hadn't planned to show them around. No sense rubbing it in with Robin. But if she was asking, Sara figured it would be OK. She pulled them from her drawer, and Erin got hers from under her bed.

"Wow!" Danielle said. "You guys look good."

148

"Super!" Becky agreed. Robin was silent. Sara was afraid to ask if she had bought any photos.

"I'll make a design of these on the banner," Danielle said, already arranging them on her bunk. "Stars of Pavlova Cabin.... Robin, do you have one?"

"Are you kidding?" she said, looking at Sara.

"Robin," Hillary said, looking at her funny.

"I said I don't have one," Robin said. "Now let's go crack-the-whip at rehearsal."

CHAPTER THIRTY-THREE

"No Name, No Finish"

Sara wondered if her dreams and imagination were bigger than she was. Dancing in the student concert with Robin and Hillary was her idea, and she was the one having trouble. "Sara, that movement is on count seven, not eight. You're always a beat behind," Robin told her. She was exhausted from trying to learn so much in one night. Her brain felt like powder and her body like a rag. Mixing the choreography and dancing it to their music was not as easy as she thought it would be.

"We have to add the final movements tonight," Robin said. "That will give us the rest of the week to get it perfect."

Miss Casey arrived and gave Sara the break she needed. "I need some info for the program notes," she said. She sat down on the floor with her clipboard, and the girls sat around her. "First, I need to know the correct spelling of your names." When they had confirmed that, Miss Casey wanted to know how long the piece was, the name of the music, and the composer. No problem. Then she asked them the name of the dance.

"We don't have one, yet," Hillary said.

"Well, let me watch you do it, and maybe we can come up with something," Miss Casey offered. Sara cringed. She was definitely not ready for Miss Casey's eyes.

"Great," Robin said getting up. They switched on the music and took their opening positions. Miss Casey watched carefully. Sara tried her best to go off balance, rebound, and get into the flow, but knew she still didn't look like a real modern dancer.

"What great music," Miss Casey said. "But you've got to fulfill it. You've got to pulse with it, you've got to make more distinctions between your percussive and sustained movements." She picked up her clipboard. "It's coming along," she said. "Let me know what the name of the dance is tomorrow." She went on to another group.

"OK," Robin said. "Let's do it again."

"But what about the name?" Hillary asked.

"I think we'll know the name when it's finished," Erin said.

But they still had no finish and no name at eight-thirty when Danielle and Becky came over to show them their jazz number. Sara wondered why she and Erin hadn't chosen something like a fun jazz dance. But she knew something fun without the technique wouldn't win a scholarship.

"What are your costumes like?" Hillary asked when Becky and Danielle were done.

"They're awesome," Becky said. "Red satin jackets and black pants."

Sara looked at Erin. They burst out laughing. "Those were our costumes," Erin said.

"I thought these were yours," Robin said, pointing at her leotard.

"Yeah, they are too," Sara laughed.

"I guess everything is yours," Robin said, not entirely lightly.

Sara watched Robin walk ahead of her out of the studio. Her beautiful hair, graceful neck, and long legs filled the archway. Everything is *yours*, Sara thought.

CHAPTER THIRTY-FOUR

"Pulse"

Tuesday they decided to go right from dinner to the studio to work on the modern piece as long as possible before Madame's first pas de quatre rehearsal. "OK," Robin said. "I'm going to flip on the music, we're going to go through it from start to finish and try to come up with the last movements. We've only got like a half a minute left, but the ending has to be perfect."

Sara agreed and got into her opening position. She thought about Miss Casey's comments and tried to express each type of move clearly. "You have to pulse with the music," she remembered Miss Casey saying. She got her inner energy going and tried to keep it going, but had no idea for an ending. No one had any ideas, and everyone wanted to work on a different part. "You guys still aren't doing our choreography right," Robin complained. "Look in the mirror and watch how we do it."

When Sara looked in the mirror, she saw something. The fit was wrong. They were trying to coax a lyrical, sustained energy into driving, pulsing music. What worked for the flute music wasn't working for the drums. Yet, it worked where the violins came in on top of the drums. Suddenly she could see their bodies representing either the drums or the violins and she had the ending. "Stop!" she said, shutting off the music. "I have it," she told them. "Robin, you're a violin. Hillary, you're a drum. Erin, you're a violin. I'll be a drum."

When she turned the music back on, she told them to improvise, taking some of the movements from earlier parts of the dance, but to invoke the quality of either a violin or a drum. She looked in the mirror and loved the contrast of the slow and percussive movements. Miss Casey came in and caught the end of it. "Great," she told them. "I like that—it's pulsing now. But you need something else. Clue: It has to do with highs and lows. But, I came to get the name of the piece."

Pulse, Sara thought. "*Pulse*!" she said, still feeling her blood pumping like the drums in the music.

"That's it!" Erin said. Hillary and Robin agreed to it.

"*Pulse*, it is!" Miss Casey said, writing it on her clipboard. "See you later."

"Wonder what she meant by 'highs and lows,'" Erin said.

"Think about it for tomorrow," Robin said. "It's time for pas de quatre."

Hillary left, and the others went to the locker room for their pointe shoes. Madame gave them an enormous amount of difficult choreography. Robin's foot was healed and she was really going for it—dancing full out and taking up more space. Sara remembered how wonderful it had been dancing for Yuri when she felt the room was hers. The pas de quatre was going to be long, with solos included for each of them. It began with the four of them pretending to skate downstage toward the audience together, their hands in the muffs. There was lots of fast and fancy footwork with échappés, relevé passés, little

156

beats in the air, and double pirouettes. Sara was exhausted in the locker room. She opened her locker door, then collapsed onto the bench, moaning. It was nine o'clock. "I feel like my mind keeps dancing after my body stops," she said. "I can't shut it off. I just hope I remember all this stuff."

"Your muscles will remember on their own," Lin said quietly. "If you let them." Sara looked at Lin. They were almost exactly the same size, yet Lin was so different. Sara wondered how she could dance so precisely and be so focused.

After lights-out, Sara went over the steps to the pas de quatre in her mind until she thought she knew them. Then she went through the modern dance piece from start to finish, hearing the violins and drums. She drifted to sleep feeling her body pulsing, touching the locket around her neck. But she dreamed there was another pearl added to the mysterious necklace that fit perfectly around her neck. In the morning, she awoke to find the chain to her locket had broken during the night. She picked up the shiny gold locket from her pillow and told herself she must have twisted it in her sleep. Feeling sad, but strangely invigorated, she put it in her drawer.

CHAPTER THIRTY-FIVE

"Pressing Petals"

Wednesday morning Miss Casey posted the program order for Saturday's dance concert. Sara was surprised to see *Pulse* listed first. Becky and Danielle's jazz number was in the middle, and Lin's Sugar Plum Fairy variation was last.

"Wow," Sara said. "We have to go out there in front of the boys first."

"We'll get it over with," Erin said.

"Yeah," Sara said. "Lin has to close the show."

"Has to?" Erin said. "It's good to be last on the program. It's like an honor to close the show."

"Oh," Sara said, taking a New Yorker's word for it.

"Actually," Robin said behind them, "it's an honor to be first as well."

"That's true," Erin said. "To open the show is just as important."

Sara felt an excitement surge through her body. Miss Casey must have liked what she had seen. She just had to win a scholarship.

That night's rehearsal was frustrating. They each had a different notion about Miss Casey's clue: highs and lows. Robin thought they should add highs and lows by changing more quickly between sharp and soft movements. Erin thought it meant the volume of the music should go up and down, and Hillary thought maybe it meant they should add some funny parts. Sara didn't have a clue. "But I know," she said, "that you guys aren't right." She convinced them to keep it the way it was, rather than go off in the wrong direction. So they simply rehearsed what they had, hoping they would understand Miss Casey's clue in time for the show.

After rehearsal, Sara decided something would have to be done about her yellow roses. They were drooping and falling off the stems onto the top of the chest, mingled with Erin's red petals. "We should press these in a book," she said.

"Here's a book," Robin said, throwing a hardback onto Sara's bed. *Dancer's Dream.* Sara turned it over to read the blurb on the back. It was the story of a high school girl who had to choose between a boy, college, or the special sacrifice of a dance career. "This looks good," she said. She gathered the fallen yellow petals and put them in the book. Erin put hers in her own book. When they were all pressed, they'd put them in the red tin.

CHAPTER THIRTY-SIX

"Sharing a Secret and Getting the Clue"

"Hurry, you guys," Hillary said to Sara and Erin Thursday after dinner. "We decided we should practice *Pulse* in our costumes tonight."

"That's a good idea," Erin said. "We can make sure our scarves aren't going to fall off."

"I don't think so," Sara said. "Do you want everybody to see our costumes?"

"They're going to see them tomorrow night, anyway," Robin said.

"I know, but I don't want anybody to see them till then," Sara said.

"But practicing in them tonight will give us an advantage," Robin said.

Sara knew she was right. She thought of something. "I know how we could wear them without anyone seeing us," she said. "Put your costumes in your dance bags and follow me." She led them carefully to the practice room in the basement where Mr. Moyne and Miss Casey had been rehearsing *Romeo and Juliet*. No one saw them go and no one was in the room. Sara knew Miss Casey was busy that night in the theater preparing for tomorrow's dress rehearsal.

"So cool!" Hillary said, shutting the door quietly.

"How did you find it?" Robin asked, turning on the lights.

It was a red tin secret they couldn't tell. Erin looked at Sara for a reply. "I got lost the first time I went to the costume room," Sara said. "It was unlocked, so I figured it would be open tonight." Her mother always told her to be careful where her imagination ended and a lie began, but Sara was sure Miss Casey would not want anyone to know about the *Romeo and Juliet* rehearsals.

"Let's get started," Erin said, looking up at the clock. "We have Madame's rehearsal tonight, too."

They felt constricted because they had to keep the music low so no one would find them, and because they had to dance in a smaller space. The turbans did fall off and they devised a new way to tie them. "Better to have stupid falling turbans tonight than tomorrow night!" Hillary clowned, letting her scarf unravel in her face.

Miss Casey's clue kept haunting Sara. Highs and lows, she thought. She watched the ending movements in the mirror. Highs and lows. Then she saw it. "I've got the clue!" she said. "Miss Casey wants us to make more interesting levels in the last part. Like we work on in modern class. You know, Robin could dance at medium level, Hillary could be lower, Erin could be on her tiptoes, and I could be on the floor." Me—on the floor, she thought. Imagine! She was becoming a modern dancer after all.

They liked the ending that way, hit on a final pose, and even fixed their bows. "I think we're ready for tomorrow night,"

Robin said. While the others were busy putting their costumes away, Sara made sure the coast was clear and opened the hall door for them.

"We do on pointe what you know first," Madame directed at pas de quatre rehearsal. "Next, I teach more."

She hit the play button on the music and watched them closely. Sara could feel Robin moving a bit ahead of the music. Lin seemed to float on top of it. Next to her, Erin went along exactly with the tempo. Sara felt like she was lagging. Madame stared at Sara's feet and clapped her hands while she shouted the ballet terms. It just made Sara more nervous, and the second time they did it she fell off pointe on the first relevé. She wished she could get behind the other girls to learn it better. But this was a pas de quatre, and this was the way Madame wanted it— all of them equal in a straight line. Sara did her best but didn't feel ready when Madame added more.

"Now you be partner with girl next to you," Madame instructed. That meant Sara and Robin were paired. They were to face each other holding hands, go up on pointe, pull back, and spin in a circle. Lin and Erin caught on right away and spun around on their pointe shoes laughing. But Robin pulled back hard on her outstretched arms before Sara was ready, so they couldn't get any momentum going. "You pull back at same time," Madame said. "Be team. Work together." The second time they tried it, Sara pulled back harder and Robin fell off her pointe shoes.

Madame looked at the clock. "OK," she said. "You will get it. Now, we go one time from beginning. On pointe, everything." They got into position and put their arms in front like their hands were in muffs. When the music began, Sara didn't know if she would make it through on pointe. With the first rise on pointe, she realized her pointe shoes were too old and soft for the difficult steps. She tried to pull up her muscles to compensate, but it was tough going. "Is coming," Madame announced when they had finished. "I begin solos next week."

When Sara took off her pointe shoes in the locker room she felt like throwing them away, her feet were so sore. She wanted a long soak in a hot tub, but a shower would have to do, followed by ointment and new Band-Aids.

"Oh, you have some blisters," Lin said, taking her own shoes off and pressing the soles into high arches.

"I know," Sara said. "I need to break in new shoes. These are too soft." But the truth was, she had just one pair of new pointe shoes left, and those would have to be saved for the final performance.

CHAPTER THIRTY-SEVEN

"Ready or Not"

Friday night by six-thirty they were backstage in full make-up and costume, warmed up and ready to go. Miss Casey's voice came through the intercom as she gave directions to the stage crew. Sara kept moving, trying to keep her muscles warm until Miss Casey called for *Pulse*.

"Let's go!" Robin hollered when Miss Casey requested them onstage. Sara's stomach jumped, as usual, and she took a deep breath hoping she'd do everything right. But rather than letting them perform the whole dance, Miss Casey kept stopping them to open up their spacing. In between, she worked with the lighting crew. By the time she asked them to perform the whole piece, Sara's muscles felt cold and she had lost the energy she started with. They were so far apart on the big stage in some parts of the dance that she missed a movement cue from Robin. That caused Erin to miss coming in on one of her sections. When they finished, there was silence except for Miss Casey talking to a stagehand through her headset. They were not excused. They reworked the spacing in two places, changed the timing on several parts, revised the choreography in one place, and then did the whole dance again.

"Look kids," Miss Casey said. "You're opening the show. You really have to send it out of the ballpark. I want more expression, more fulfilling the music. Let's go again."

"Not bad," was all she said when they finished. "Stick around for final bows." She called the next group.

"I don't think we're ready," Sara said in the dressing room. She felt like she needed five more rehearsals to get it perfect.

"It will be fine," Erin said. "It's only for fun, anyway. Can't you just have fun?"

"Yeah," Hillary said, letting her headscarf unravel again and dancing her clown steps from *Les Patineurs*. But Sara didn't laugh. It would only be fun to her when they got it right.

"Guess what!" Robin said. "Ready or not, the show's going on!"

"Well, let's at least rehearse it some more back here," Sara said. After getting drinks they went through the piece as best they could in the hall several times, then even Sara was exhausted. They went to watch Danielle and Becky's jazz number from the wings, and congratulated them when they were done. The boys would like it.

Finally, Lin took the stage. Everyone came running and squeezed in the wings to watch. Miss Casey let Lin go all the way through it the first time, and no one breathed during her whole performance. She had waited so long and yet was as light, lyrical, and wonderful as if she had gone first. The soft lighting made her seem to glow like she was dancing inside a halo. Her dark eyes and shiny lips sparkled like the beading and ribbon on the pale lilac costume. She was delicate, but strong in her technique. When she finished, an outburst of applause filled the theater. All Sara could do was stare in wonder.

Lin bowed as beautifully as she had danced, then stood on the stage in her glistening costume waiting for Miss Casey's direction. "OK," Miss Casey said, smiling. "That's a wrap." She called everyone back to the stage to practice a final group bow, and then released them. "Everybody's tired, so go right to your cabin and get some sleep. It's going to be a great show!" Miss Casey applauded them and everyone joined in the clapping, adding whistles and cheers. "Make sure you're in your dressing room by six o'clock tomorrow for the seven-thirty curtain." The dancers left through the wings and jumped off the front of the stage. Sara caught Lin and praised her performance, but Lin was not happy. "It was OK," she said. "I have to keep working."

"Looks like the boys are having a bonfire," Erin said as they crossed the dining hall lawn. Sara looked across the lake. By this time tomorrow night the show would be over, and she and Hank would be eating ice cream and dancing together. She could still feel how warm his hand was when he had held hers in the woods.

CHAPTER THIRTY-EIGHT

"The 50ᵗʰ Lakewood Student Dance Concert"

"All dancers to the green room!" Miss Casey's voice beamed through the dressing room intercom.

"The what?" Sara asked. It was nearly seven-fifteen, and she wanted more time to stretch before the performance.

"Green room," Erin said. "It's just a room where you get a pep talk before a performance."

Sara put on her lipstick, checked her costume one more time in the mirror, and followed the other dancers. They found Miss Casey in a large room off the backstage hallway. If the walls were green, you couldn't tell because they were covered with posters from student dance concerts from years past. Sara's eyes wandered over the splashy graphics: "Lakewood Student Performance - 1978!" and "The Best of Lakewood - 1964!" "Young Dancers of Lakewood - 1988" and "Lakewood Dancers - 1990!" In each one there were photos of costumed dancers smiling.

A photographer came in and climbed up a ladder in the corner behind Miss Casey. "Everybody scrunch," Miss Casey directed. Sara moved closer to Erin and pictured this year's poster on the wall with the others. Even if she never returned, her picture would be here. She smiled into the camera wondering what had happened to all the girls in the posters. She hoped years from now when a young Lakewood dancer saw her picture, she'd recognize her as a famous ballerina.

"Now, everybody hold hands," Miss Casey said. Then she told them to squeeze hands on the count of three. "This is for you-know-what!" she said, not wanting to say "good luck" in case it brought bad luck. "Let's go for it," she said. "*Pulse* on stage!"

From behind the curtain Sara could hear the boys talking, and when the music started and the curtain opened, they shouted in excitement. The house was packed. She could see Madame and Miss Sutton in the front row. Her heart started beating too fast, making her body stiff. She was doing the movements correctly, but not expressing them fully. She caught Miss Casey's eye in the wings and remembered what she had said about being first on the program. She had to help knock this number out of the ballpark. She caught a glimpse of Robin fully confident and relaxed, and saw Erin smiling. She remembered Hillary joking with her headscarf unraveled. She smiled and began to breathe with the dance. By the end she was just sorry she had wasted the beginning movements when she could have really fulfilled them. A performance was certainly a one-time thing.

If it wasn't perfect to Sara, the boys loved it. They filled the theater with noise to the ceiling as the girls took their bows and ran offstage. Sara caught her breath and took off her headscarf.

The music from the second dance number came through the intercom, and Sara was glad all that was left for her was the final bow.

"That was dynamite!" Robin said. "We nailed it."

Sara and Erin watched Danielle and Becky's jazz dance from the wings, and hugged them when they ran off. It was terrific, and the boys let them know it.

"Come on," Erin said when it was time for Lin to go on. "Let's get our stuff organized so we can get right to the party." Sara gathered her things from the counter and put them into her dance bag. She put the headscarf back on for the final bow. Lin went out the dressing room door, and the Sugar Plum Fairy music filled the room through the intercom. Soon a senior came to get them. "Everyone in the wings for final bows!"

Sara kept trying to steal glimpses of Lin around everyone's heads. The boys were as quiet as the girls had been at last night's rehearsal. Sara thought it looked amazing from what she could see. After Lin's curtsie, Sara rushed onstage with the group for final bows. Then the curtain closed, ending the 50th Lakewood Student Dance Concert.

"Let's hurry," Erin said, moving toward the dressing room to get her make-up and costume off. But as Sara brushed her hair, she was surprised to see tears in Lin's eyes. "Ready?" Erin asked, tossing her dance bag over her shoulder.

"You go ahead," she told Erin. "I'll be there in a minute."

"You were beautiful," Sara told Lin when the other girls had gone. "What's wrong?"

"I didn't do it right," Lin said quietly, sitting in her chair. She looked down as she slowly took off her pointe shoes. "I missed a part."

"You couldn't tell," Sara said.

"I made something up," Lin sniffled. "I couldn't do it. It was too difficult for me."

Sara realized Lin was after perfection and nothing less. She understood. "Lin, hardly anybody our age could do that part at all, let alone dance it perfectly." It was true. Besides, Lin was the only dancer who had attempted a variation from a real ballet.

"But, I've been dancing since I was six years old!" Lin said, as if she were a complete failure.

"Even so," Sara said, "that variation is hard."

"Thank you," Lin said. "I'll be better now. Maybe I'll get it in ten years." She managed a smile.

Sara finished dressing for the party and waited for Lin. On their way out of the empty dressing room, she remembered to grab three programs from the show and put them into her dance bag. As they rounded the corner to the dining hall they could hear music and laughter coming from the windows. "I'm not going to the party," Lin said. "I am too tired." She gave Sara a hug, and took the path to her cabin.

CHAPTER THIRTY-NINE

"Unexpected Performance"

A crescent moon hung low over the lake and the stars seemed to shine in the lawn in front of the dining hall. Sara almost expected the creatures from *Swan Lake* to appear. She thought of the handsome prince who would be true to the Swan Queen forever. Hank was just inside the door.

She dropped her dance bag into a pile in the corner and looked around. Erin and Paul were in a crowd of dancers in the center of the room, and Becky and Danielle were eating ice cream cones on the sidelines. She waved to them and got in line for ice cream, scanning the room for Hank. David came up behind her. "What a great performance!" he grinned. His teeth looked whiter, his hair blonder, and his tan darker with the passage of summer. "No kidding," he said. "You were awesome!"

"Thanks," Sara said. "A lot of it was Robin's choreography."

"But you danced it," he said, approaching the ice cream counter. "What's your pleasure? Pink, green, brown, or pure white?"

Sara looked again for Hank. "Strawberry," she said. They carried their cones to the circle of spectators watching the

173

dancers. David was trying to say something, but the music was too loud. She went up on her toes and he bent down and spoke into her ear.

"I loved that music you danced to," he said.

Her eyes suddenly found Hank. He was in the far corner talking with Robin. Her long legs crossed under shorts, she looked like a rock star in a halter top, her hair falling around her shoulders. Sara watched as Robin took Hank's hands and led him onto the dance floor. The music changed to a slow song, and she saw Robin smile into Hank's face as they swayed to the tune. He isn't even looking for me! Sara thought.

"What was that music?" David said into her ear.

"I'll write it down for you," Sara said. I have paper in my dance bag."

She started toward her bag, but David caught her hand. "Wait," he said. "We can do that later."

But Sara sure didn't want to stay and watch the dancing. She tossed the rest of her cone into a trash barrel and looked at David. "Let's go for a walk," she said. They strolled onto the dock looking up at the stars. Sara's heart hurt that it was not Hank next to her. David put his arm around her. "David," she said, slipping away. "What about Robin?"

"She looks busy to me," he said.

"Yeah," Sara said, feeling tears. "I have to get back," she said, walking toward the lawn. David followed her and stood next to her as she found her dance bag.

"Can you give me the name of that music?" he asked.

Sara tried not to look across the room. If she saw Hank and Robin again it would not be good. And even if Hank came over something would be spoiled. "Sure," she said, finding paper and pencil.

"Let's go sit on the porch," David said.

Sara couldn't wait to leave. They sat on the porch steps in the light of the window while Sara wrote down the name of the music and the performance group. When she handed it to David, he kissed her. No arms, no hands, just a kiss. "Sara?" It was Hank. Robin stood next to him. "Where have you been?"

Sara's lips felt like a neon sign from David's kiss. "Here," she said. "Watching." She looked at Robin. "There's been a lot to see."

"Yeah," Robin said. "Especially out here."

Sara felt as jumpy as the torch flames dancing at the lake. "Not really," she said. "I was just going to the cabin." She stood and held her dance bag securely on her shoulder.

"I guess you've had enough fun for one night," Robin said.

David said nothing. He was absolutely no help. Sara was angry and embarrassed. "Well, I've had enough for one night," she said, walking down the steps.

"Sara, wait," Hank said.

But it was too late. Everything felt inside out and backward like the choreography got mixed up. Like the curtains opened and people were dancing the wrong roles. Sara went to the empty cabin and shut the door. She felt like she was under a wicked magician's spell, like the Swan Queen floating alone on the pond. Well, I don't need any prince to rescue me, she thought. If he can't be true, it wouldn't break the spell, anyway.

She got the red tin from under Erin's bed and threw it onto her bunk. Then she pulled a student dance concert program out of her bag and put it in the tin. She went to her drawer, got the program from *Les Sylphides* and dropped that in, too. She looked at the yellow rose petals on the chest of drawers, scooped them up and put them on her bed. She got Robin's book out from under her pillow and shook the pressed petals into the tin. A piece of paper fell out and landed on top of the rose petals. She unfolded it, and read:

July 28

Dear Sara,

We watched a pink sunset smear over the sky with you at the fire and me so nearby.

Torches were yellow-orange, fiery and bright, your eyes a reflection of their glowing light.

We walked in the woods among tall, rustling trees, and I held your hand in the cool and dark breeze.

Dancing together, your cheeks a fine blush—the blue stars were twinkling especially on us!

You danced like a gentle wind blowing a sail, into cool waters, your dance will prevail.

I'll be the billowed cloth touched by your charm, enchanted by sailing with you on my arm.

Hope I'll see you again soon,
Hank

"What?" Sara said to the empty room. "I don't believe this!" What was Robin doing with Hank's poem to her? She read it again. So that was why he asked her on the horseback ride if she liked poetry. I told him I wasn't into it, she remembered, that I was only into dance. July 28, she thought. She pulled the boys' party flyer out of the tin and checked the date: Saturday, July 23. She counted forward to July 28. It was Thursday, the night before *Les Sylphi*des dress rehearsal, the night she went into the woods looking for Erin, the night Robin fell through the plank. "The night Hillary saw a man walking away from the cabin," she said out loud.

The door opened and Erin came in. "What's going on?" she asked. "Are you OK?"

"If the truth really does set you free," Sara said. She explained everything to Erin.

"I need to go back to the party and find Hank," she said.

"Too late," Erin said. "He left as soon as you did." They heard someone coming. Sara put the poem under her pillow, and Erin threw the red tin back under her bunk.

Robin and Hillary came in. "Sara," Robin said. "What's wrong with you?"

"Me?" Sara said. "You were the one dancing with Hank."

"You were the one kissing David!" Robin countered.

"He was the one kissing me!" Sara said. "And what is this?" She pulled out Hank's poem.

Erin and Hillary stared at Robin. "I found it stuck in the cabin door the morning after I sprained my foot. I was the first one up, going to the nurse."

"Why didn't you give it to Sara?" Erin said.

"I don't know. I was so angry about my foot," Robin said.

"And now I'm so angry about Hank!" Sara said.

Danielle and Becky hollered through the screened door. "Robin! David's looking for you!"

"Oh.... I'll tell him to explain about the poem to Hank," Robin said in a huff. She and Hillary left.

Sara sighed, put Hank's poem under her pillow, and gathered the rose petals from her bed to press in *Dancer's Dream*. My life is more like *Dancer's Nightmare*, she thought. But when she opened the book, the first sentence she read was, "She knew that dance was more important to her than anything else." Sara thought the words were meant just for her to see tonight, and felt herself grow stronger inside.

CHAPTER FORTY

"You Must be Together"

Monday morning Madame finished class forty-five minutes early, and sent them down the hall for their *Les Patineurs* costumes. "Photographer here at ten o'clock," Madame said, pointing up at the clock. "Change quick, come right back!"

At ten the studio was filled with swirling velvet skirts, white hats and fluffy hand muffs. It was odd to have your picture taken when you didn't even know the dance yet, but this way they would have the photos back in two weeks when camp ended. "Red here, blue there," Madame ordered, clapping her hands and pointing. "White in center." Sara smiled for the photo, wondering if her picture would be in next year's Lakewood brochure. She just had to win a scholarship.

They waited their turn while Madame quickly organized poses separately for each of the smaller groups. The pas de quatre was last, and by the time they had finished, Class B was crowding the doorway in their costumes. "OK, you excused now!" Madame said over the confusion. "Take costumes back. Tomorrow, regular class!" Sara looked into the mirror and did a

179

quick pirouette to see how far the skirt would flare out around her. The layered net petticoat danced by itself under the beautiful white velvet. She didn't want to take it off. She saw Madame approaching in the mirror, but it was Lin Madame spoke to.

"You do well in show," Madame told her. Lin looked down at the floor. "Not perfect, but was good." She smiled broadly at Lin. "One day you will be getting it, don't worry! Keep trying, yes?" Lin nodded. Madame lost her smile and looked at Sara and Erin. "You do fine, too." With that she waved for Class B to enter the studio. Sara made her way through the girls, disappointed that she could not have impressed Madame the way Lin had. She wondered how she'd look dancing next to Lin in the pas de quatre. She was going to have to work hard. "You do fine, too," she heard Madame saying again. But it had sounded to Sara like a crumb given out of politeness. As she pulled her costume off, she tried to imagine what it would feel like to have Madame smile down at you the way she had smiled at Lin.

In modern class Sara felt Miss Casey pushing her, expecting more. "Hit that movement, Sara! Really punch it!" she coached. During the slow adage work she pulled Sara's leg up higher, throwing her more off center, lifting her leg out from her body. It nearly knocked Sara over, but she felt the expectation of the position for the first time. It felt wonderful, like learning to read. Maybe her body was beginning to take on the shape and flow of modern dance at last.

"See!" Madame shouted over the music at pas de quatre rehearsal that night. "Is why you must be together!" She shut off the music. "You will get. Keep trying." But the spin with Robin just wasn't happening. They were supposed to flow into it from the previous fast steps, but Robin was always standing there with her hands outstretched waiting for Sara.

"Can't you hold back a little?" Sara whispered to Robin.

"Can't you get up to tempo?" Robin asked.

"OK, girls," Madame said, looking at the clock. "Do from beginning on pointe. Then I add more." The music began and Sara glided downstage with the other three dancers, pretending her hands were in a muff. After the fast footwork Robin was in position for the spin again before Sara. She took Sara's hands and spun her awkwardly.

"Now repeat same steps and spin again," Madame said. "Do section twice!"

Great, Sara thought. She looked at Robin. "Speed up," Robin said.

"Slow down," Sara said. But it was no use. During the fast footwork, Sara sensed Erin dancing at tempo, Lin floating above the music, and Robin moving a bit faster than the music, as usual. Her own movements were a little lagging, she knew, but her pointe shoes were getting softer with each rehearsal, making it more difficult. Now, as Madame was demonstrating the next movements, Sara's toes were throbbing.

"We learn more tomorrow," Madame said. When Sara took her pointe shoes off, she was relieved to feel her squashed feet expand in the air.

CHAPTER FORTY-ONE

"This Requires Magic"

"You should have told us that door was broken!" Robin said.

Sara turned from the banner. "What door?" she asked. She stood back and looked at the artwork. Erin had drawn figures representing *Pulse* next to Becky and Danielle's drawing of their jazz number. Sara was putting the final touches on the words arching over the whole banner: "Leadership, Cooperation, Enthusiasm, Improvement". The *Les Sylphides* photos shined from the edges. She couldn't wait for Becky and Danielle to see it.

"That door by the secret practice studio in the basement," Hillary said. "We were stuck in there forever." It was almost time for lights-out.

"What were you doing there?" Sara asked.

"We heard music coming from the room and saw Mr. Moyne and Miss Casey rehearsing *Romeo and Juliet*," Robin said. "You didn't tell us about that either."

"Didn't tell you about what?" Danielle asked as she and Becky came in.

"Nothing," Sara said. "Just an old room we found to practice in." She was afraid everyone at Lakewood would find out.

"Wow!" Becky said. "The banner looks great. Pavlova is the best cabin!"

"Yeah," Robin groaned, throwing down her dance bag. "The best."

The next night at rehearsal, working with Robin seemed even worse. The spin could only work if they both arrived at the same moment, pulled back equally hard, and balanced each other's weight. Sara danced as fast as she could to arrive at the same time, but Robin was still getting there first and pulling Sara into an awkward spin. Madame moved on to the next part. "Now do sit spin," she said, "With partner." She demonstrated with Lin and Erin. They did it easily, with Lin holding Erin's hand above her head while Erin twirled down close to the floor and back up again, ending in a supported arabesque. But when Sara and Robin tried it, Sara slipped off her pointe shoe to the floor.

"Must support each other!" Madame told them. "Try again." But again Sara ended up on the floor. "Hold her up," Madame said to Robin. "Pull up when she goes down. And Sara to come up quicker from bottom. Don't stay down." She sure wasn't trying to stay down, but Robin wasn't pulling her arm tight, and it didn't help that Sara's shoes were so soft.

Wednesday after lunch Erin refused to practice her tap in the cabin. "It's too hot," she said. "Besides, I'm going to row out and see if Paul will come out on the lake."

Sara practiced a few modern dance movements on her own, then took out her last pair of pointe shoes. She stared at the shiny pink satin. They would have to be broken in perfectly for the final performance. Everything depended on it. She took the silky ribbons out of the shoebox, along with a needle and pink thread. She thought of wearing the shoes that night to pas de quatre rehearsal, but knew if she did they'd be too worn for the performance. She got on her bed with the pointe shoes and pulled Hank's poem out from under her pillow, feeling something else. The *Swan Lake* concert program was still there.

She lay back and looked at Yuri's picture again. She flipped the pages until she found the picture of Yuan Wu. She closed her eyes and tried to feel what it would be like to raise her leg as high as Yuan could, to be lifted far into the air by Yuri, to be so lyrical and light. She felt around her neck for the pearls connecting her to all of classical ballet. She opened her eyes to see that the program had opened to a page quoting Balanchine on Romantic Ballet: "To be romantic about something is to see what you are and to wish for something entirely different. This requires magic." The last time Sara had felt magic was in the mysterious cabin in the woods. She grabbed her dance bag and put in Hank's poem, the *Swan Lake* program, her new shoes and ribbons, and the red tin.

The little deer jumped over the rivulet of water with Sara and stared at her as she pushed open the cabin door. Sara found a window that opened and let in the fresh air. She put Hank's poem and the *Swan Lake* program into the red tin and pushed it under the old bed. Then she sat in the middle of the floor and sewed her ribbons into her pointe shoes. When she was done, she placed them carefully under the bed to soak up the magic.

CHAPTER FORTY-TWO

"Lin's Shoes"

After folk class Sara was rushing to change for dinner when Erin handed her a note. She threw her character shoes into her locker and opened the folded paper:

August 18
Sara,

> *David told me you never got my poem until Saturday night.*
> *I wonder if you liked it. Could I see you soon?*

Hank

"How did you get this?" she asked Erin.

"Paul brought it out to my boat this afternoon," Erin said. "I think Hank feels bad."

"Yeah," Sara said. "But the poem doesn't erase his flirting with Robin."

"Sara," Erin said. "I'm your friend, right?"

"My best at Lakewood," Sara smiled.

"Well, I have to tell you that you aren't perfect."

"What do you mean?" Sara said.

"I mean David rescued you in the lake, David hugged you after horseback riding, David kissed you Saturday night."

"I know," Sara said. "But I couldn't help it."

"Maybe Robin couldn't help it, either," Erin said shrugging.

Sara felt betrayed by Erin. And she still felt angry about Robin and Hank. She couldn't sort it out. She wished she could claim an emergency at the dance office and call Jen at home. She carried her confused feelings with her to pas de quatre rehearsal after dinner.

"You must learn everything— solos—everything by week from tonight," Madame said. "Dress rehearsal next Thursday, final performance Friday." And the announcement of the scholarship winners, Sara thought anxiously. "Must improve and cooperate to accomplish," Madame told them. "You can do. Will be fine."

But Robin still seemed to be speeding to Sara so that the circle spin was still off balance, and Sara couldn't get up from the bottom of the sit spin in time to do the arabesque on the right count. Madame charged ahead with their solos, starting with Lin, giving her the perfect fancy footwork to showcase her talent. Sara couldn't wait to see what her own solo would be like. "OK," Madame said. "We take it from top, then Sara get solo tomorrow night."

It turned out to be amazing! The large waltz movements and flowing music filled Sara with joy. "You take whole stage," Madame told her. "Is bigger, bigger than room!" Sara smiled in delight as she pictured herself in the white velvet costume dancing across the big outdoor stage. But when Madame asked her to try the movements on pointe, Sara had trouble with her old shoes. They were barely supporting her, and her toes were squashed and hurting. "Need new shoes now," Madame said. "You wear tomorrow."

"All right," Sara said, not knowing what she'd do.

"But I don't have any more pointe shoes," she said to Erin in the locker room. "I have to save my last pair for the final performance."

"Take these," Lin said quietly, handing Sara a shoebox from her locker.

Sara opened the box to find a brand new pair of pointe shoes exactly her size. She didn't know what to say. "Are you sure?" she said. "I mean, don't you need them?"

"No," Lin smiled. "I want you to have them."

Sara touched the ribbons and felt a lump in her throat. "Thank you!" she said, hugging Lin.

"Thank you for talking to me after the student concert," Lin said. "That's when I noticed we wear the same size." They hugged again, and Sara thought of the shoes she'd left in the mysterious cabin. Now she knew they'd be safe there until the final performance.

CHAPTER FORTY-THREE

"Follow Me"

Friday, Sara took a sandwich to the cabin for lunch and ate it while sewing the ribbons in Lin's pointe shoes. It was her only chance to do it, with Madame's pointe class at one o'clock and the day filled with classes after that. After dinner they had pas de quatre rehearsal, and Saturday was *Les Patineurs* with Class B. To get a scholarship, I still need more time to practice modern technique and my solo, Sara thought. With just one week left until the final performance and rehearsals day and night, time was almost up.

The new shoes were too hard at pas de quatre rehearsal that night to do her any real good, and Robin simply refused to slow down. "Team work!" Madame shouted at them. "You cooperate together. Timing. Balance!"

Sara's feet worked their way into blisters during her solo rehearsal. "That's one way to find out where you're going to need Band-Aids," she whispered to Lin while Erin was learning her solo. But at least she got an idea of how the performance would feel danced full out on pointe. Now she could work on fulfilling it.

"I love my solo!" Erin said after rehearsal. She was overjoyed with all the pirouettes in place and traveling turns around the stage. "I feel like I'm really skating!"

"I feel like I can't even walk," Sara said, feeling the blisters.

Saturday Madame kept them past noon for *Les Patineurs*, then told them to come back after lunch. Sara's head felt stuffed with all the new steps and patterns, and she blanked out on part of her solo. "You can do flat, you can do on pointe." Madame told her. But it wasn't true. She had no trouble remembering it while wearing her soft ballet slippers, but the minute she tried it in her pointe shoes, she blanked out.

"I'm jinxed," she said to Erin as they watched Danielle dance her part.

"No way," Erin said. "It will come to you Monday after we get some rest. Remember Sunday, the day of rest?" She helped Sara up and they ran onto the floor to rehearse the first section of the ballet. Again, the sliding out in pairs onto the stage went well, but the big circle kept breaking apart. Madame was frustrated.

"Is Saturday, yes?" Madame said. "Is five days to Thursday dress rehearsal. You come back tomorrow after lunch. You get this. Not to worry. We work!"

"You remember Noday?" Sara said to Erin. "Day of no rest?" Erin shrugged.

"Please stop pulling away from me!" Robin whispered to Sara. So far, Sunday rehearsal wasn't any better than Saturday's. The big circle was breaking up again.

"I have to keep up with Erin," Sara said, her fingers barely hanging on to Erin's waist. The music kept its frolicking pace, Madame kept pouring on the choreography, and the dancers kept struggling to remember and perform. The circle had to stay intact, and the girls in the pas de quatre had to end up in front of the audience and that was all there was to it. Sara was relieved when Madame skipped the pas de quatre and taught the whole group the final section.

"Robin in center," Madame said. "Lin, Sara, Erin, Kathy on her sides." Little by little all the other dancers joined the lines as they pretended to skate around like a wheel. Soon the entire room was filled with a giant pinwheel spinning around like the dancers were performing in the Ice Capades. Sara imagined the bits of snow falling on them, the white costumes in the center. It was going to be awesome. On the last count of the music, Madame set a pose with the end girls kneeling, the middle girls in a curtsie, and the pas de quatre dancers on pointe. Robin stood in the center smiling, her feet and arms outstretched. Her parents would be so proud of her, Sara thought.

"My parents aren't coming," Robin said at dinner. "They never do. And I really don't care because we're going to look stupid if you don't get your timing right."

"Me?" Sara said. "I am going as fast as I can. And you aren't keeping my arm straight in the sit spin."

"You'll get it," Erin said. "We just have to keep practicing."

"This is Sunday night," Sara said. "We can only keep practicing for so long. Then the curtain goes up!" She thought of her mom in the audience. If she didn't get a scholarship, maybe her mom could get the money from her dad if she looked great in the performance. That was really a long shot. Oh, I have to get a scholarship, she thought again.

"We're going for a quick swim while David's still on duty," Becky said. She and Danielle left. Sara thought it might be easier to like horses or swimming more than dance.

But she knew she had no choice. The ribbons of passion tied her to pointe shoes.

In the cabin with Erin, Sara stared at the banner. "Leadership, Cooperation, Enthusiasm, Improvement" she read. She heard Madame saying they'd have to cooperate and improve to learn *Les Patineurs* in time for the final performance. You can't cooperate alone, she thought. Robin's going to have to do her share.

"Hey, where's the red tin?" Erin asked, looking under her bed. "I have to put the rest of my flower petals in."

"I put it in the old cabin in the woods," Sara said. "For safe-keeping. I left my last pair of pointe shoes there too. We can put your petals in when we get my shoes."

Hillary and Robin jumped on the porch and opened the screen door. "David says hello," Hillary said to Sara. "I think he likes you." Robin frowned at her.

Sara felt more awkward than she did trying to get up from the bottom of the sit spin. She felt like she was trying to circle spin with Robin and it was the same old tugging and pulling. Then anger filled her, and words seemed to fly out of her mouth on their own. "I don't care," she said. "I don't care who likes who."

"Of course you don't," Hillary said. "Because Hank and David both like you."

"I seriously don't care," Sara said sternly, looking Robin in the eye. "We have a performance to do. I'll be dancing with you, not Hank or David."

"I can't trust you," Robin said.

Sara didn't know what to say. Anger and frustration rolled through her body. A scholarship, dance, her life hung in the balance. They were going to have to get it together. They were going to have to pull as a team. They were going to have to dance in a circle of power. This would require magic. Sara felt something come over her and felt the pearl necklace tugging at her. "Get your dance bags and follow me," Sara said, ready to break a red tin promise.

CHAPTER FORTY-FOUR

"HERS"

Sara led them to the secret path making sure no one saw them. She twisted left after crossing the rivulet of water and led them to the old cabin. "Now don't speak," she told them. Silence would be part of the ritual. She pushed opened the door and motioned for them to sit on the floor. They brushed away the acorns and sat in a circle.

The old skillet on the wall seemed to watch as she continued the ceremony. "Everyone take their performance shoes out and put them in the center," she whispered, her anger magically replaced by determination and focus. The diminishing sun bathed the cabin in a gentle light.

"Can I just ask if we're off-limits?" Hillary whispered.

Sara got up, motioned for them to move over and made a line with the acorns, dividing the cabin in half. "If we stay on this side of the line," she said, "we're on the girls' side. Now put your pointe shoes in the middle and close your eyes." She watched while they obeyed, then got her own performance shoes out from under the old bed and put them with the others. She held her hands above the pile of shiny pink pointe shoes and closed her eyes. "Take a deep breath," she said, feeling the pearl necklace and the sacred ground beneath the shoes. "We call the spirits of the dancers of old to be with us," she said. "All the great dancers that ever were, tell us your secrets. Help us to perform as one." Hillary snickered. "Hillary is called upon first," Sara said.

"What do I do?" Hillary asked, holding back laughter. Erin nudged her.

"You say a word," Sara told her, making it up on the spot. "You say a word using the first letter of your name that will give us power. Say the letter first."

"H," Hillary said. "Hooray! Hooray for us!"

"Yes," Sara said. "The spirits of old dancers accept that. Now Erin."

"E," Erin whispered. "E for enchanted dancing."

"Yes," Sara said. "The old spirits like it. Now Robin."

But there was only silence. Sara could see that Robin's eyes were closed, but wondered if she would speak. Robin fidgeted, and Sara thought she might leave the group.

"R," Robin finally said. "Remarkable. Remarkable achievements for us all!"

"Great," Sara said, relieved. "Now me. S. Success. And scholarships for those who are meant to receive them from the old dance spirits." She waited a moment touching the secret pearls around her neck. "Now hold hands and each of us say our letter in order." When they had stated their letters, she realized it spelled HERS. "H. E. R. S.," she announced. "This is the HERS pact of power and magical dancing. We are one in team-work and one in dance. We put our performance and friendship above all else. We repeat this together."

The girls repeated, "We are one in teamwork and one in dance. We put our performance and friendship above all else."

"We thank the spirits of the dancers of old for coming," Sara said. She looked around the circle. "Now open your eyes."

Everyone blinked and looked at the others. "Hooray for HERS!" Hillary said, holding her pointe shoes in the air.

"Hooray for HERS!" they all repeated, raising their shoes. Sara thought all four pairs of dance shoes had taken on a special glow. She wasn't sure how she had thought of any of it.

CHAPTER FORTY-FIVE

"The Muffs Mess Things Up"

By Tuesday night's rehearsal something better was happening. It wasn't performance level yet, but Robin seemed to be slowing her tempo a bit. "It isn't me," she said when Sara thanked her. "I think you're going faster." Maybe, Sara thought.

She practiced the pas de quatre in the corner with Lin and Erin while Robin learned her solo. "It is perfect for her," Lin smiled when they sat under the ballet barre to watch. Robin's legs seemed even longer as she swirled them around and over her head pretending to skate. She seemed to soar near the ceiling in her leaps.

"Now all come," Madame said, waving them center-floor. "Robin finish last leap here. You in straight line together and do pirouette, pirouette, double pirouette until last count of music. Sara looked at Lin. She could never do this step without Lin's shoes, but they were not exactly right for her, and the blisters were still rubbing. She was glad when they had done the set of turns four times and finished on one knee. "Big smile!" Madame said.

201

Wednesday morning Madame had reserved the big studio for *Les Patineurs* rehearsal with everyone together. "Take muff to opening position," she said, pointing to a box of the fluffy white muffs in the corner. It was tricky to transfer the muff from one hand to the other as the dance steps demanded. "No giggle!" Madame told them as they made mistakes handing another dancer a muff instead of a hand. "Everyone to have muff on outside hand when hold waists in circle skate. Audience can see." But it made it even more difficult to hang on to Erin's waist, and Sara could feel Robin's hands slipping away from her. "We get right today," Madame said, repeating the music over and over. She made corrections to their spacing until the circle began to hold. But the pas de quatre dancers ended up on the side of the circle instead of the front when it stopped. "Again!" Madame said. When they got it right, Sara wondered if it was just luck.

"Change your muff next time!" Robin whispered to Sara as they began the sit spin. "I can't hold your hand up."

"No! No!" Madame yelled, pointing to Sara. But she let the music go through to the end of the dance. "OK," she announced. "We have work to do, but no more days. You come back here after break. Other teachers say is OK." After lunch, Robin forgot to push her muff up for the circle spin with Sara, so Sara felt fur instead of flesh and nearly fell over. And though Sara remembered to switch the muff for the sit spin, Robin was late in pulling her arm tight.

"A letter from your mom!" Erin said, tossing an envelope to Sara after dinner.

Erin had already read hers. "My parents can't wait to see the final performance," she said.

Sara ripped open her letter. Everything was fine. Her mom would be in the audience Friday night. "Jen is looking forward to your coming home," she wrote. But home seemed so far away. And the performance seemed too close with so much to get right before the audience took their seats. She thought of the concert programs she had saved in the red tin for her mom and Jen. She looked at the banner and the photos of *Les Sylphides* and Yuri. She wasn't sure she ever wanted to go home. She looked again. There was a photo of Robin in a frothy white costume—her *Les Sylphides* picture! She had put it on the banner with the others.

Madame only kept them for pas de quatre until eight that night. "Is coming," she said. "Get rest tonight. More rehearsal tomorrow, then dress rehearsal at night. You will do!" Sara rubbed her feet in the locker room. She was going to have to get her performance shoes from the old cabin and wear them all day tomorrow and Friday to get them just right for the final dance concert.

"We're going to the laundry room," Danielle said, gathering her dirty things.

"Yeah," Becky laughed. "My parents threatened to leave me here if I smelled like sweaty leotards or horses!" They threw pillowcases of dirty clothes over their shoulders and left.

"I have to go to the office and call my mom," Hillary said, folding a letter. She jumped down from her bunk. "Want to come, Robin?"

Robin was on her bed writing something. "No," she said without looking up.

"I'll go," Erin said. "Come on, Sara." She put her letter in her drawer and opened the screen door.

"That's OK," Sara said. "I'll stay here." She felt under her pillow and pulled out the note from Hank. *Could I see you soon?* she read. Too late now, she thought. But she pictured his dark tousled hair and blue eyes, his dimpled smile. She shoved the note into her pocket and climbed down from her bunk.

"Where are you going?" Robin asked as Sara opened the door. "Can I come?"

Sara looked at Robin's picture on the banner and thought of their HERS pact. "Sure," she said.

CHAPTER FORTY-SIX

"Do You Think It's Important to Win?"

"There's the Will-O-Way," Robin said looking out at the lake.

Sara saw Hank and Paul sailing around a buoy. "They're out late," Sara said. "It'll be dark in an hour."

"There's David," Robin pointed. He was cutting through the water in a motorboat. Robin turned to Sara. "I have to tell you something."

"What?" Sara said.

"I think David was flirting with you to get back at Hank because of losing the sailboat races."

"What?" Sara said. "How do you know?"

"That's what Hank was talking to me about at the ice cream party," she said. "He said David was really angry, that he couldn't seem to take it all as fun. Hank told me winning shouldn't be that important."

Sara remembered her conversation with Hank the day of the horseback ride. Sara had said she thought winning was important, that sometimes it could change your life. Hank had said sometimes your life can change if you don't win. "Do you think it's important to win?" she asked Robin. "That it can change your life?"

"Yes," Robin said. I want to win a Lakewood scholarship more than anything."

"But your parents send you here every summer anyway," Sara said.

"No, they don't," Robin said. "My grandmother does. My parents send me to a boarding school during the winter while they travel on business, and my grandmother sends me here in the summer so I don't have to stay in the city with her. But if I won a scholarship, I'd be coming here on my own. I'd be sending *myself* somewhere. If I won a Lakewood scholarship my parents would not only come to a performance, but they might actually send me to a high school for the arts where I could dance every day!"

"Come on," Sara said. She led Robin to the secret path and on to the mysterious cabin. They opened a window and sat on the bed. Sara reached under the sagging mattress and grabbed her pointe shoes.

"Did you leave those here the other night?" Robin asked.

"These are the ones I saved for the final performance," Sara said.

"You better break them in," Robin said. "Put them on."

Sara pulled them on over her thin white socks and wrapped the ribbons tight. She stood up and felt her toes adjust perfectly. She pushed her arches over as far as she could and felt the shoes support and lift her. "Oh," she sighed. "These are perfect! I can do anything!" She turned in circles around the room and stepped into an arabesque. Robin caught her hand.

"Let's try the circle spin," Robin said. She took Sara's hands and they spun around. "Now let's do the sit spin." Sara corkscrewed down to the floor while Robin held her arm and brought her back up into a pose. "Great!" Robin smiled.

"But we're not using muffs, and you don't have your pointe shoes on," Sara reminded her.

"I know, but let's keep practicing," Robin said. "Here. Use my sock for a muff."

Robin went barefoot, and they hummed and counted and practiced until it was nearly dark. Then they collapsed. Sara took off her pointe shoes and held them to her chest. Robin put her shoes back on and stood up. "Look!" she said, motioning Sara to the window. The little deer stood in the woods staring back at them under the whisper of a moon.

CHAPTER FORTY-SEVEN

"August 26 in the Year of Summer Dance"

"Are rough spots, but is working," Madame announced at Thursday morning rehearsal of *Les Patineurs*. "You have teamwork together. Need with Class B now. All together after lunch. Come right back."

Sara thought of her great plan to practice modern dance with Erin during breaks after lunch. It seemed to have disappeared like a waterfall over a rock among all the ballet rehearsals. At four o'clock when they finally got to modern class, Sara wondered if she had improved enough to qualify for a scholarship. She had only today's class and tomorrow's to show what she could do.

"Reach into space!" Miss Casey yelled at Sara as she moved through the room. "Show me the difference between soft and sharp! Show me!" The second time her group danced across the floor Miss Casey stopped the pianist. "Watch this group," she told the class. "Some of them are really nailing this combination." When the music began, Sara threw herself into the movements, but she couldn't tell if she was one of the dancers nailing it. "OK. Next group," Miss Casey said after nodding a general approval. Maybe I'll nail something tomorrow, Sara thought. But at the end of class Miss Casey told them they would not have modern dance or folk class Friday. "You get the afternoon off to rest before the performance," she said. "So thank you for a great summer. You were all wonderful students." It's over? Sara thought. She applauded for Miss Casey with the others, and bowed to her in thanks for her whole summer of training. "See you at dress rehearsal tonight!" Miss Casey said as they filed out the door for the last time.

"It's over," Sara said at dinner. "I have no more chances in modern."

"You looked good in there today," Erin said. "Really."

Sara looked at her. "Is it like in ballet, where if you get a lot of corrections, it means you show potential?"

Erin looked into her water glass. "I'm not really sure with Miss Casey."

"Special delivery for Pavlova table!" Mary said, passing out large envelopes. "One for everybody." Sara pushed her plate aside and opened the clasp. 50th *Lakewood Student Dance Concert* it said on a shiny folder. Inside was the group picture the photographer had taken from the ladder. The beautiful painted leotards and headscarves stood out, and Sara smiled back at herself. The performance had gone well. She looked at Lin in the corner of the photo in her shimmering Sugar Plum Fairy costume. How sad Lin had felt that her performance was not perfect. "To be romantic about something is to see what you are and to wish for something entirely different," she remembered. Balanchine said it required magic, but Sara knew it also required years of hard work.

210

"Why are you putting your picture up there?" Becky asked Danielle in the cabin. "We'll just have to take it down tomorrow." Sara looked over to see Danielle taping her student dance concert photo to the banner.

"Well, it isn't tomorrow yet," Danielle said.

"Yeah," Sara said. "It isn't tomorrow yet." She gathered her stage make-up, tights, and performance shoes and left with Erin for the big outdoor theater on the lake. Their dance bags jiggled on their shoulders as they climbed the tall steps to the dressing rooms.

"In here!" Hillary called to them. Sara saw her name listed on the door with half of her class.

"The seniors got that big dressing room down the hall by the stage," Robin said. "But look out here." She went to the back of the dressing room and pushed a steel door. It opened onto a narrow railed balcony that overlooked the lake.

Sara and Erin walked out into the crisp air. "Wow," Sara said. The lake was rippled by the wind, surrounded by tall green trees, and framed by an evening blue sky. "This is like the first time we saw the lake from the lookout bench," she said to Erin remembering how they had laughed when a chipmunk scurried out from under the bench, and how they ran back together for the opening ceremonies.

"I will never forget this moment," Erin said dreamily. "August 26th in the year of summer dance!" They hugged.

"Come on, you two," Robin said. "Get into your white velvet. We have to warm up."

Soon the room was filled with dancers in mostly red or blue velvet trying to pin their white hats securely to their hair. "Here are your muffs!" a senior hollered as she pushed a box into their room. "They were in our room by mistake." All the

211

intermediates from the other dressing room came to get one. It seemed like pure chaos to Sara. She still had to get warmed up and go through the steps in her mind. She checked her eye make-up, put on lipstick, and grabbed Erin.

"Where's Lin?" Robin asked.

"Already downstairs in the wings," Hillary said from under a funny crooked hat.

"The pas de quatre should stay together," Robin said. "Wait for me."

They found Lin watching Mr. Moyne and Miss Casey practicing *Romeo and Juliet* onstage. "So beautiful," she said. "I didn't know they were going to do this."

"I can't wait to see it," Sara said, excited that she'd get to see the performance all the way through.

Madame gave them permission to warm up standing in front of the stage while the crew discussed lighting for *Romeo and Juliet*. Sara kept staring off into the open view of the trees and lake. There was a roof over the hundreds of seats in the audience, but no walls. It would be magical as the sky darkened around the theater and the stage lights became bright. By the time they sang the Lakewood song, the moon would be lilting above the lake. She worked her muscles and went through the sequence of switching the muff from hand to hand, and when the juniors went onstage she stood in the wings next to Erin.

"Look! Here's a program," she said, reviewing the pink and black paper taped to the wall. The juniors were first in *Folk Dance Fantasy* by Mr. Moyne, followed by *Les Patineurs* staged by Madame Landovsky, then the seniors in *Mozart in Pink* by Miss Sutton. The balcony scene from *Romeo and Juliet* would be last. Sara sighed. It was going to be an amazing evening.

"Let's go through the pas de quatre in the hall," Robin said.

Sara was watching the juniors twirl to lively music in red skirts with green and yellow embroidery. Long ribbons flowed down their backs as they hit their tambourines over their heads. She turned away and followed Lin and Erin. They performed the steps as best they could in the narrow hallway, then they were called to the stage.

"We stage pas de quatre," Madame said. "Next everyone all together!"

"*Les Patineurs* ready in the wings," a voice said over the intercom. Sara could hear all the pointe shoes clicking on the floor as the dancers gathered.

Their music began suddenly. "No!" Madame shouted. "Give me eight bars before!" Sara felt nervous and tiny on the huge stage. Her costume felt too tight now, and she was afraid her hat was loose. "OK!" Madame said. "You go this time."

You go, Sara thought as she put her hands in her muff and pretended to skate downstage with Erin, Lin, and Robin. Madame stopped them over and over, directing them to space themselves out across the stage. When the time came for Sara to dance her solo, she had lost the flow, and she blanked out in the same spot she had in the studio. "We go on!" Madame shouted, calling for Erin's solo. They pushed through to the end, landing on one knee and smiling. Sara felt like crying. How could she have blanked out again?

"Opening places for *Les Patineurs*!" Madame said, clapping her hands. Sara and Erin ran to the girls waiting in the corner and crossed arms. They held their hands tight as the music started and they led their line onstage. But the stage was so big, they were late in meeting Robin and Lin's line for the big circle. They began again. At least the pas de quatre ended up in front, and Madame let them dance the whole ballet through. When the dance was over, she moved them through certain sections for spacing, staged their bows, and excused them. "Think!" she said. "You must remember timing and spacing tomorrow night. Think about it! You can do!"

Sara's heart was heavy as she made her way through the seniors waiting in the wings in their gauzy pink costumes and hair ribbons. The juniors who had been watching *Les Patineurs* were jumping around in the hall. "You were so good!" a little girl said to Sara. She smiled up at her like Sara was Yuan Wu and had just danced *Swan Lake*.

"Thank you," Sara said. When she smiled down at the young dancer, she felt her own heart open. Maybe everything would be OK. "Let's stay here and watch the seniors," she said to Erin. The little dancer stood in front of her in awe at the swirl of pink on the stage. When it was over Mr. Moyne called for the child, and Miss Sutton called everyone onstage to organize closing ceremonies.

"Seniors in back," Miss Sutton said. "Intermediates next, and juniors in front." She switched a few people around so the taller girls were in the middle. "Look around and remember where you are," she said. "I'll be at a podium over there." With a list of the scholarship winners, Sara thought. Her shoulders felt chilled. She just had to win a scholarship. "Your parents won't be able to meet with you until after the closing ceremonies. They'll meet you at your cabin so we don't have everyone backstage. Thank you! Be here tomorrow at six."

Everyone cheered and headed for the dressing rooms. Sara was glad to get out of her costume. She hung it carefully on the clothes rack next to Erin's. Her hat felt awkward and heavy. She unpinned it, made sure her name was in it and in her muff, and set them under her costume. "Ready?" Erin asked, taking concert programs for them.

Not really, Sara thought. "Ready," she said as they left for their last night's sleep in Pavlova cabin.

CHAPTER FORTY-EIGHT

"Paper Memories"

"It is now three o'clock!" Sara said. "We have to be at the theater by six."

"Yeah," Erin said. "That gives us three hours to do nothing."

"That gives us three hours to do *everything*!" Sara said. "And we have to eat dinner at five." Madame had given them a regular ballet technique class in the morning, and Mr. Moyne took them through their paces in both tap and folk after that. From one until after two-thirty, Madame rehearsed *Les Patineurs* with both classes, and then set them free. In the hall, they had picked up photos of *Patineurs*. Now Danielle was putting them on the banner.

"I can't believe you're doing that," Hillary said. "We have to take that down."

"Not yet," Becky said.

"Not yet," Erin repeated.

Not yet, Sara thought wistfully. She grabbed her suitcase out of the closet. "I can't pack!" she said. "All my clothes are dirty."

217

"I think we should all go for one last swim," Hillary said.

"I think we should all go for one last horseback ride," Becky laughed.

"I think we should all clean up this cabin," Danielle said.

"I think we should all be quiet," Robin said. She was on her bunk writing something again.

"I'm going to the laundry room," Sara said.

"I'll go with you," Erin said, grabbing her things. When they got back, the cabin was empty and strange. It was as though they had already vacated the premises. Suitcases and bedrolls lay on top of exposed mattress ticking, and the drawers and closets were empty except for Erin's and Sara's things.

"We better get packed," Sara said. But she felt a force pushing at her, making this the last day of Lakewood against her will. They folded everything neatly into their suitcases and rolled up their sleeping bags. Sara put *Dancer's Dream* on Robin's bunk. Erin reached under her bed and pulled out her last pair of pointe shoes. Sara found the crumpled note from Hank in her pocket. "The red tin!" they said together. "Hurry!" Sara said, heading out the door. Erin scooped up the last of her fallen red petals and followed.

They emptied the tin in the middle of the old cabin floor. Letters, flyers, notes from the boys, concert programs, and red and yellow flower petals lay before them. Sara threw her last note from Hank into the pile, and Erin sprinkled it with her flower petals.

"What's your best memory?" Sara asked, touching the student dance concert flyer.

"*Swan Lake*. Definitely *Swan Lake*," Erin smiled. "What about you?"

"Yuri. Definitely Yuri," Sara laughed. Oh, she thought. If I could just dance in his class every day . . . . They divided everything into two piles to take home, according to ownership. "Who gets the tin?" Sara asked.

"You do," Erin shrugged. "It's yours."

But Sara didn't feel that way. It was something they had shared all summer. "Not really," she said. "It belongs to both members of the Red Tin Club!"

"Well, someone has to take it," Erin said.

"What if no one takes it?" Sara said. "What if we leave it here for next summer?"

"Next summer?" Erin said. "I'm not positive I'm coming back, are you?"

"I won't be, unless a miracle happens," Sara said. "But if I don't and you do, you'll have it."

"And if I don't and you do, you'll have it!" Erin said.

"Now, where should we put it?" Sara said, looking around. Not under the bed, not behind the old skillet. A deer hunter might come. She looked up at the ceiling. "There!" She got on the wobbly chair and climbed onto the table. Erin put all the flower petals back inside the tin and handed it to Sara. Sara hid it snugly in the old wood rafters. Cobwebs would grow over it by winter.

The dinner bell rang out across the lake as they gathered their paper memories and closed the door behind them.

CHAPTER FORTY-NINE

"Final Performance"

"Take your photos!" Danielle said as she finally took them off the banner after dinner. Sara put hers in her suitcase next to her paper memories from the red tin. She chose what she would wear after the performance that night and placed it neatly in her dance bag.

"Help me fold the banner somebody," Danielle said. Sara's eyes traveled over the colorful figures representing their roles in *Les Sylphides*, *The 50th Lakewood Student Dance Concert*, and *Les Patineurs*. "Leadership, Cooperation, Enthusiasm, Improvement," she read. She knew their meanings now and felt she had worked hard to live up to them. Becky handed her the folded banner. She put it in the suitcase and zipped it shut.

"Let's go!" Mary said from the porch. She hugged each of them as they went out the door to the theater. "Break a leg," she said.

In the dressing room Erin handed her camera to Danielle, and the pas de quatre posed in their fluffy white velvet and fur. Sara was so excited she felt like her bright red lipstick popped off when she smiled. Erin took a shot of Becky, Danielle, and

221

Hillary. "How will I send you these pictures?" Erin said. "I need to get your addresses." There was no time now.

"I have them," Robin said. She handed them each a white paper heart with red trim. "Lakewood" was written in the center. Sara opened hers. In the inside were all of their names and addresses, including Lin's.

So that's what she was busy doing on her bed, Sara thought.

"How did you get our addresses?" Erin asked.

"Mary got them from the office," Robin said. Lin hugged her.

As Madame came into the room, Robin whispered for Hillary, Erin and Sara to look on the back of the heart. "HERS" it said. Sara choked back tears as she said thank you and put the heart on the dressing counter under bright lights.

"Everyone to come in this room," Madame said. All the intermediates squeezed together. "You learn dance well. Is yours now. Dance and have fun!" she said. "The summer goes quick. Tonight goes quick. All take hands." Sara put her hands into Erin's and Robin's. "I count three, and you say 'Ura! Ura!' In Russia means 'Hoorah!' Cheer for *Les Patineurs.*" On the count of three everyone raised their arms into the air and shouted "Ura! Ura!"

"*Folk Dance Fantasy* onstage!" the stage crew voice hollered over the intercom. "*Les Patineurs* in the wings!" Sara adjusted her hat and checked her shoe ribbons to make sure the stitches were solid. She looked into the mirror wondering if she'd return to the dressing room a scholarship winner. In the wings she stepped into the rosin box and kept moving her legs to keep her muscles warm. When the juniors took their bows she threw her sweater and leg warmers into a corner and took a deep breath. She was so excited she was afraid she might laugh out loud as she stood with Erin, arms crossed, ready to lead their line onto the enormous stage. The applause was thunderous for the juniors' folk dance, making Sara worry she wouldn't hear the beginning of the *Les Patineurs* music. But as the juniors rushed off stage past them, there was a silence that seemed to fill with Sara's heartbeat. Then the music began and Sara and Erin danced onstage in perfect unison. Her mother was out there somewhere.

The rows of seats were filled with families and friends who applauded as the dancers pretended to skate in the big circle. All fifty muffs going around on the outside while the girls danced the lively steps must look wonderful! As Sara glided downstage with Lin, Erin, and Robin for the pas de quatre, she worried she would blank-out on her solo, but she kept dancing. Her enchanted shoes worked perfectly as she and Robin partnered in the quick circle spin, and the audience cheered as she came up from the sit spin into the arabesque pose. Lin performed her solo with exquisite movement and grace, and as Sara moved forward to dance her own solo, she remembered what Lin had told her: "Your muscles will remember on their own if you let them." The large and flowing waltz music filled the air and she simply moved with it. As she let her muscles remember, she seemed to take up the whole stage, and her smile reflected the joy in her heart. The audience rewarded her with long applause as she danced into the background and tried to catch her breath. Sara's eyes followed Erin as she performed her solo.

As Erin's traveling turns took her stage left, Sara saw Madame watching them from the wings. She pulled herself up a little taller, imagining again how it might feel to have Madame smile down at her in approval. Then Erin took her place next to Sara, grinning at the applause, and Robin began

the swirling leg movements and leaps Madame had choreographed especially for her. Sara watched Robin's long legs reach
higher than the red hair tucked under her hat, and thought
how much Robin had overcome after her sprained foot to arrive
at this moment. "Great!" Sara whispered as Robin finished and
stood next to her for their series of pirouettes. Sara's perfect
pointe shoes took her solidly through the single and double
turns in place, and she knew she was dancing in unison with
the others. As they landed on one knee, the audience burst into
applause again, and she caught a glimpse of her mother smiling
at her from her seat near the stage. Sara's heart skipped as she
smiled back.

Hillary's clowning brought waves of laughter; Danielle's
solo brought appreciative applause, and Becky's crack-the-whip
caper brought cheers for the group. As Sara moved into the center of the stage for the grand pinwheel finish, the snow began to
fall. Bits of white paper brushed Sara's face as she watched the
snow swirling onto the hats and shoulders of the other dancers. It must look beautiful to the audience—fifty dancers in
blue, white, and red velvet under falling snow in summer. The
snow fell harder as the pinwheel became larger and picked up
speed. The audience rose to its feet in cheers as the dancers
ended precisely on the last beat of the music. Sara smiled and
held her pose next to Robin in the very center, legs and arms
outstretched. As soon as the curtain closed in front of them,
Madame motioned for them to clear the stage quickly. Sara ran
off between the stage crew sweeping up the paper snow.

"That was great!" Erin said as they made their way through
the senior dancers waiting to go on.

"Yeah," Sara said. "Madame is a genius! She knew we could
do it." She felt expanded by the performance just as she had

after dancing in *Les Sylphides*. She knew how much she had changed, how improved her dancing had become. She knew Lakewood had changed her life.

Once the seniors moved onto the stage, Sara and Erin joined the others quietly watching them dance from the wings. As entertaining as *Les Patineurs* might have been, it couldn't compare to the level of technique and grace of *Mozart in Pink*. "Look at them," Sara whispered. "They are fabulous!"

"You will be too," Lin whispered behind her. "We must keep working."

Sara sighed. When the curtains closed on the seniors, they ran back into the wings and joined everyone else straining to get a good view of Mr. Moyne and Miss Casey. The couple practiced a supported pirouette behind the curtain while the crew pushed the balcony onto the side of the stage. Miss Casey climbed to the top of it over Sara's head, and Mr. Moyne waited across the stage. Sara was enchanted the moment the music began. Romeo was as romantic as a prince as he courted Juliet from afar, beckoning her down from the balcony. They were a dream of white flowing around the stage. She danced away from him, let him catch her, and danced away again. Their love was forbidden because they were from rival families, but Romeo risked all for her. Now she leaped into his arms, and he let her fall backward brushing the floor. He lifted her above his head and they swirled in joy. When Juliet ran back up to the balcony, Romeo leaped onto the outside of it and climbed to her. Juliet leaned over the railing and they kissed as the music ended. The girls screamed in praise.

Mr. Moyne and Miss Casey took their bows in front of the curtain to waves of applause. Sara watched as Miss Casey received a bouquet of flowers and bowed graciously. Romeo and Juliet bowed to each other, and Juliet took a flower from her bouquet and gave it to Romeo. Sara gasped in delight. Mr. Moyne held the flower elegantly as Miss Casey bowed again. They ran off stage and the audience finally grew quiet.

"Places for closing ceremonies!" the intercom voice directed.

CHAPTER FIFTY

"Closing Ceremonies"

The curtain opened on the last evening of Lakewood's fiftieth summer of dancers. Sara's heart leaped as she saw Miss Sutton at the podium across the stage. She felt the seniors breathing behind her and the juniors squirming in front of her. On either side, Lin and Erin felt electric.

"Thank you for coming and supporting these wonderful dancers!" Miss Sutton said to the hundreds before them. "We've had a summer of excitement and growth. We've learned to dance alone and together, to step in for each other and to cheer for each other, to lead and to follow. And while so many of these dancers deserve the honor of a scholarship, we could choose only three from each division." Sara felt like she might explode waiting.

Miss Sutton reached for her paper. "The junior winners are," she said. As she announced each girl's name they walked to the center of the big stage, the audience cheered, and the dancers squealed and hugged. Mr. Moyne presented a bouquet to each one, and Sara was delighted to see that one of the winners was the little girl who had complimented her own dancing. "The intermediate winners are," Miss Sutton began. Sara held her breath and closed her eyes as Erin and Lin squeezed her hands. "Third place, Kathy Jacobs." Sara let out her breath and cheered as Kathy made her way to center-stage. Then she closed her eyes and waited for the next name. "Second place, Sara Sutherland." Sara nearly fainted. She cried as Lin and Erin crushed her with hugs. I can't believe it, she thought as she walked on shaky legs to take her place next to Kathy. She was so buoyant with joy, she thought she might fly off the stage. "First place, Robin Stewart," Miss Sutton said. "Robin!" Sara cried, watching Robin walk toward her. You'll send *yourself* to Lakewood next summer, she thought as Robin stood next to her beaming. But she realized there was no award left for Erin.

Sara felt engulfed in cheers and applause as she watched Madame walk toward her with an armful of flowers. She looked up to see Madame smiling down at her in a streaming light of approval. When Madame handed her the bouquet, Sara felt her heart open like all the flowers in it opening at once. Her whole body danced in the pinks, yellows, and reds of the pet-als as she curtsied to Madame one last time. When the senior winners joined them, the photographer took a few quick shots. Sara would be in next year's Lakewood brochure! She had won a scholarship.

"Congratulations to all our scholarship winners," Miss Sutton said. "Now I have a surprise. The San Francisco Ballet visited us this summer, and I'd like to introduce Yuri Pashchenko from the company." Yuri! Sara watched in awe as Yuri walked from the audience to the stage. He had seen their whole performance!

"Hello," Yuri said when the screams subsided. "I enjoy per-formance very much. Lakewood has many fine dancers this year.

But only one I have to choose for scholarship to San Francisco Ballet School."

Sara was astonished—someone would actually be dancing for Yuri, someone ready to move on to be part of a real company school. Please let it be Erin, she thought, knowing it would probably be a senior. Please let it be Erin.... Please let it be Erin.

"Winner is intermediate dancer, Lin Tan." Lin! Sara had forgotten about Lin in all the excitement. Now Lin walked gracefully to the middle of the stage and curtsied for Yuri as he handed her a bouquet with flowing ribbons. When Yuri gave Lin a hug, Sara felt her own heart flutter. She looked over to see Erin clapping and cheering.

"I can't believe," Lin said, standing next to Sara. But it was true. Lin would be trained from now on by world-class teachers and have a chance to get into the company some day.

"It is true," Sara smiled. She would keep the pointe shoes Lin had given her and follow their pink shine to her own success. As the music began for the Lakewood song, Sara cleared her throat and hoped the words would come out around the lump of emotion.

Lakewood, Lakewood nestled fair
among the leaves and northern air.
We come to you to dance and share,
to grow and learn, to teach and care,
to make new friends and build new paths,
which lead us on to dreams that last.
And when the summer's days are through,
we'll think of our return to you
and never once throughout the year
forget our friends made steadfast here.

Sara broke into sobs as the song ended and the curtain closed in front of them. She made her way toward Erin wondering what Lakewood might be like next summer without her. They threw their arms around each other. "Congratulations!" Erin said. Then they were in the middle of a crowd of dancers. She hugged Lin and Hillary, Becky and Danielle, and hung on to Erin in the crowd. She found her warm-up clothes where she had thrown them, but didn't see Robin anywhere. "Wow!" Danielle said. "Hoorah for Pavlova cabin!"

"Ura for Pavlova!" Becky said. "Ura! Ura!"

There was so much confusion on stage, Sara wondered if they'd ever make it to the dressing room. "Come on," she said to Erin when she found an opening. They made their way toward the hall among the chaos and were half way up the stairs to the dressing room when Robin caught up to them.

"Sara," Robin said. "You have a visitor at the stage door."

"Go ahead," Erin said. "I'll see you in the dressing room."

Sara thought her mom had gotten mixed up about where to meet her, but when she opened the door, Hank stood there. His blue eyes twinkled like the stars behind him, and his smile caressed her face.

"You were wonderful!" Hank said. "Congratulations."

"I didn't know you'd be allowed to come over," Sara said.

"Mr. Field said it would be OK for a little while." He looked at the concert program in his hands. "I really like dance," he said.

"I really like poetry," Sara said, remembering Hank's note. She took a long flower from her bouquet and gave it to him. He bent down and gently kissed her cheek.

"See you next summer," he whispered as he walked away.

Sara stood a moment in her costume watching him, then looked down at her flowers and turned back into the theater. In the dressing room, she looked into the mirror and touched her cheek. She went to the back of the dressing room, opened the door to the balcony, and walked out into the night air. She looked at the burst of silver stars dancing overhead, and gazed across the lake to the thick August forest she knew hid the trails, the stream, the little deer, and the mysterious old cabin. She breathed in the smell of pine, thought of the ancient dance spirits, and felt a chill as something light as a whisper caressed her neck. Moonlight brushed her hand as she reached for the string of pearls she saw floating toward the stars. "See you next summer," she whispered back.

Glossary of Dance and Theater Terms

Apron
The part of the stage nearest the audience. The dancers generally do not dance on it.

Adage
Slow and graceful movements performed with control and ease.

Allégro
Brisk, lively steps.

Arabesque
A pretty pose. The dancer stands on one leg with the other leg in the air behind.

Barre
The horizontal wooden or metal bar fastened to the walls of the ballet studio that the dancer holds for support.

Battement
Beating step.

Body positions
Movement through poses in different positions.

Bourrée	Quick, tiny running steps on pointe.
Chassé temp levé	A slide into a hop in the air.
Choreography	Dance steps or movement phrases.
Choreographer	A person who composes dance steps or movement.
Contraction	A contracting of the muscles of the diaphragm.
Corps	Same as ensemble. The group of dancers who do not solo.
Downstage	Toward the audience.
Demi	Half or half-pointe.
Derriére	Behind, back.
Développé	Developing movement. The gesture leg points to the knee, then extends out away from the body.
Échappé	Escaping, level movement of both feet to second or fourth position.
Emboité	A little jump turning, with boxed, tightly fitted feet.
En tourant	In turning. The dancer turns while dancing.

En diagonale	In diagonal. The dancer movers on a diagonal.
Gesture leg	The leg that moves.
Grand or Grande	Large or big movement.
Grand Révérance	Large curtsie.
Grand battement	The gesture leg is raised quickly from the hip and lowered with control. Like a high kick to the front, side, or back.
Jeté	A jump from one foot to another from a brush.
Passé	The gesture leg passes in front or back of the supporting leg.
Pas de bourrée	Bourrée steps. Or, for example, moving one foot back, the other side, then the other front.
Pas de deux	Dance for two.
Pas de quatre	Dance for four.
Piqué	The dancer steps directly onto pointe or demi-pointe.
Pirouette	A turn on one foot.

Plié	Bent, bending. A bending of the knees to make the joints and muscles pliable and soft, and the tendons flexible.
Relevé	Raised. A raising of the body onto the balls of the feet or onto pointe.
Retiré	The dancer brings the toe of one foot to the knee of the other foot.
Scrim	A thin curtain stretched across the stage to produce a mysterious or shadowing effect when the dancers are behind it.
Spotting	The movement of a dancer's head during a turn. The head is the last to leave and the first to return to a spot in front of the dancer on a directed path.
Stage-left	The dancer's left when facing the audience.
Stage-right	The dancer's right when facing the audience.
Supporting leg	The leg that holds the dancer's weight when the other leg moves.
Tendu	The gesture foot slides out to the front, side, or back, and back again.
Tombé	The weight of the dancer falls onto one leg.

Upstage   Away from the audience.

Variation   A solo dance in a classic ballet.

Wings   The sides of the stage out of the audience's view.

What Do You Think?

Point of View

1. From whose point of view is this story told? (Which character?)

Setting

1. Where is the setting of the story?
2. Why is the setting important for the main character?
3. Think of two ways that the northern woods challenges the main character.
4. Think of two ways that the dance setting challenges the main character.

Description

1. Can you find an example of how the author describes what the main character looks like?
2. Can you find an example of how the author describes what one other character looks like?
3. Can you find an example of how the author describes the personality of the main character?

4. Can you find an example of how the author describes the personality of another character?
5. Can you find an example of how the author describes the setting such as the cabin, the dance studio, or the dining hall?
6. Can you find an example of how the author describes the natural (woods) setting?

Symbols

A symbol in a story is something that has a deep meaning, like the locket.
1. Can you find examples of two symbols in this story?
2. What does the first symbol mean?
3. What does the second symbol mean?

Plot

A plot is what happens in the story.
1. What happens in this story? Can you BRIEFLY tell the beginning, the middle, and the end?
2. What would you say is a turning point in the story? That is, when the plot takes an important turn that might change the outcome of the story?
3. An ending should be expected, based on what we know of the characters, but should also be a bit of a surprise. Can you tell in what way this ending was expected?
4. Can you tell in what way this ending was a bit of a surprise?

The Characters

1. Who is the main character?
2. Who is the second most important character?
3. Who are some other important characters?

Sara was glad her mom left before she ran into her cabin mates.

1. Does it mean Sara doesn't like or love her mom?
2. What does it mean?

Sometimes Sara's dad sent the child support payments and sometimes he didn't.

1. What does this tell you about Sara's family?
2. How might this make Sara's life different from some of her friends?

Sara's boyfriend took someone else to the spring dance because Sara was busy rehearsing for her dance concert.

1. What does that tell you about Sara?
2. What would it mean if she went to the dance instead of rehearsal?

During auditions, Robin seems to force Sara first to the back line, then to the front line.

1. Is this fair?
2. Was Robin just doing her best, or was she being mean? Was it up to Sara to fight for the place she wanted to be? How could she have done this?

Robin acts like Sara pretended to drown to have David rescue her.

1. Do you think this is true?
2. Why would Robin act this way?

Erin tells Sara that Madame corrects her dancing a lot because Madame sees talent that needs to be developed.

1. What does this let you know about Sara's ability?
2. What does his let you know about Erin?

Sara is uncomfortable practicing Robin's part. She is actually glad that Robin will be dancing the part and not her.
1. Do you think Robin is worried that Sara will get her part? How do you know this?
2. Should the way Robin feels stop Sara from trying her best?
3. Do you think Robin would ever guess that Sara really doesn't want to dance her part?

Sara thinks Robin and Hillary are wearing too much make-up to the boys' party. She tells them they are not going to perform, that they don't need "stage make-up."
1. Why do you think Sara would say this?
2. Was Robin respectful of Sara when she called Sara "the incredible shrinking ballerina" in the costume room?
3. Was Sara respectful when she told Robin and Hillary they didn't need "stage make-up" ? What is going on between them?

Sara and Erin go to the old cabin in the woods. They're not sure if it's off-limits or not.
1. Was Sara right in thinking that it would be OK to go there as long as they used the cabin to practice dance?
2. Why is important to the girls to have a secret place to go?

Sara goes out after lights-out to find Erin because she believes Erin might be in trouble.
1. What else could Sara have done?
2. Was Sara to blame for what happened to Robin?

Sara is told she will dance Robin's part. Dress rehearsal is that night with the performance the next night.
1. Robin might think Sara is happy about getting to dance the special part. Is she?
2. Sara decides to go back and try her best at dress rehearsal. What other choices did she have?
3. What would have happened to her if she had made a different choice?

Sara feels their student concert dance must be better than Lin's, Robin's, and Hillary's. She is so desperate about this that she gets in an argument with Erin.
1. Why does Sara feel so strongly about being the best?
2. Why does Erin leave in anger? How else could Sara have let Erin know her feelings?
3. If Sara had not gotten angry, might Erin have been supportive of Sara's feelings and goals rather than run away?

Sara discovers that Robin and Hillary plan to wear the same costumes in the student dance concert. Instead of giving in or continuing the argument, Sara suggests the four of them dance together in the same costumes.
1. Do you think this was a good suggestion?
2. What else could Sara have done?
3. How did all four dancers learn more about dance from this solution?
4. How did they learn more about themselves from this solution?

Sara takes the girls to the practice room in the studio basement where Miss Casey and Mr. Moyne rehearsed *Romeo and Juliet*. But she does not tell them that she saw their teachers secretly practicing there.

1. Why didn't Sara tell the whole truth?
2. Who or what was she protecting?

Sara is eager to get to the ice cream party to see Hank, but stays behind to comfort Lin.

1. Why was this important to Sara?
2. What does it tell about the things that are most important to Sara?

At the ice cream party, Sara sees Hank dancing with Robin. She is hurt and decides to leave. She walks on the dock with David. David tries to put his arm around her, then kisses her as they sit on the porch. Hank and Robin see the kiss.

1. When Sara saw Hank and Robin dancing, what other choices did she have besides leaving the party?
2. Once again, there's friction between Sara and Robin. They just can't seem to get along very well. Who caused the problem this time?
3. How do you think Sara could have handled herself differently after the kiss?

Sara finds a poem in Robin's book addressed to Sara from Hank written the night of the boys' party.

1. Do you think Robin has any good excuse for not giving it to Sara?

   Why or Why not?

2. Does Robin make things right by saying she'll tell David to explain to Hank that Sara never got the poem?
3. What do you think Sara is thinking or feeling when the book falls open and she reads, "She knew that dance was more important to her than anything else"?

Erin tells Sara she's not perfect, that some of the problem between Sara and Robin has been Sara's fault.
1. Was that a good and helpful thing for Erin to do?
2. What risk was Erin taking by telling her that?

Lin gives Sara a pair of her pointe shoes.
1. Why did Lin do this?
2. How did it make Sara feel?

Sara feels angry and pushed beyond her patience when Robin and Hillary say they think David likes Sara, and Robin says she doesn't trust Sara.

She can't take any more. As a response to her own anger and frustration, Sara decides to try to rise above the petty arguments and to try to bring them closer together by performing the ritual in the secret cabin.
1. What other way could Sara have behaved as a response to her deep anger and frustration?
2. Do you think Sara was courageous in performing the ritual in the cabin? If so, why?
3. Did Sara have any previous success in this story with bringing the group together? If so, when?
4. Do you think that previous experience helped her in this situation?

Robin tells Sara she wants to win a Lakewood scholarship more than anything. Her parents and grandmother send her off to boarding school and to Lakewood, so she is never really home. But she loves dance and wants to send *herself* to Lakewood next summer.

1. Why is it important for Robin to send *herself* to Lakewood?
2. Might Sara and Robin have been friends all summer if they had had this talk at the beginning of summer?

Sara takes Robin to the secret cabin in the woods. Robin works with Sara so they can dance better together.

1. When Sara and Robin really get to know each other, what happens?

Miss Casey keeps pushing Sara to go beyond what she's doing in modern dance class.

1. Why do you think Miss Casey is doing this?
2. Has Sara earned this attention? If so, how?

A young dancer compliments Sara. When Sara says "Thank you," and smiles down at her, she feels her own heart open.

1. Why would Sara feel that way?
2. Why is it important for older dancers to pass down the skill and passion for dance to younger dancers?

Near the end of the story Sara feels she understands the meaning of "Leadership, Cooperation, Enthusiasm, and Improvement," and feels she has worked hard to live up to them.

1. Do you agree?
2. Can you think of some examples from the story that show Sara learning about these things?

After the final performance, Sara knew that Lakewood had already changed her life.

1. Sara thought she'd have to win a scholarship to feel changed. Why does she know her life has already changed?
2. If she doesn't win a scholarship, will it be the end of her dance adventures?

Lin wins a scholarship to the San Francisco Ballet company school.

1. How does this make Sara feel?
2. What does Sara do or think in the story that lets you know Lin is a role model for her?

Sara stands on the balcony alone after the final performance. The make-believe string of pearls connecting her to the old tradition of classical dance seems to float from her neck toward the stars.

1. When Sara says "See you next summer," do you think she's speaking to the ancient dance spirits or to Hank?
2. Why do you think the make-believe pearls left her at the end of camp? What will she have to do to get them back?

CPSIA information can be obtained at www.ICGtesting.com
Printed in the USA
LVOW071502010812

292534LV00011B/120/P